Pippin Pearmain is enjoying the busiest week of her life. As a child star turned jobbing actor, she's used to tight deadlines and patient waiting around, but this return to the world of stage and film after ten years of unofficial retirement is a whole new experience. Filming Half-Life of the Lost would be enough for most sixty-something women, but Pip also has to attend the world premiere of her ballet, *Delphine*, and dance the principal role in her second ballet, *Queen of the Clowder*. A grey leotard with a stocking tail and Alice-band ears is fine for a costume, but Pip ends up with a glorious silver crown. For someone who doesn't do jewellery, she seems to be accumulating quite a lot! She has new friendships to cultivate and, as the sunset falls on her most challenging film role ever, she has a strange encounter that's been fifty years in the making.

Back home in quiet Jellico Bay, Pip joins a new friend in a mad expedition to her childhood home to fulfil a promise. Along with her film co-star and two peculiar cats, Pip creeps into the garden under a full moon . . .

Performing Pippin Pearmain 7
Copyright © 2023 Lark Westerly
ISBN: 978-1-4874-3721-3
Cover art by Martine Jardin

Published by eXtasy Books Inc

Look for us online at:
www.eXtasybooks.com

Performing Pippin Pearmain 7

By

Lark Westerly

Dedication

For those of us who do what we love and who love what we do —
may it ever be so.

Author's Note

Fiction and Reality

Major places in the story, such as Tasmania, the city of Sydney and the state of Victoria do exist. So does Bass Strait. The towns of Jellico Bay and Delmsford are made up, as is Delphinium Island. The suburb of Windhill is made up. If it existed, it would be somewhere near North Sydney. The suburb of Glebe is real as is the iconic Sydney Harbour Bridge. The children's book Georgia Kemble references in the chapter Pizza is Noel Streatfeild's Party Frock, (1946).

Pip's story covers a year, taking her from her reclusive cottage in Jellico Bay to her old hometown of Delmsford, to the magical fossmere, on to Sydney and thence to Delphinium Island. The nine books compile into one continuing story, slowly revealing the mystery and magic that has been part of Pip's world all along.

And how did I come to write Pip's story? It all began with a flower show . . . and with a bucket.

The story so far . . .

Book One

Introducing Pippin Pearmain — small, eccentric, determined, sixty-six, and ruled by cats. Until a decade ago, Pip earned her living by playing offbeat roles on stage and screen, but after her mother and her agent died in the same week, parts dried up and she moved to Jellico Bay. During a visit to her old hometown she encountered her cousins, Lupin de

Leon and Juniper "Jan" Sharman. They, and Jan's daughter, Clarkia, were the only remaining members of the Laurel-Pearmain-de-Leon family. Over afternoon tea at the Delmsford Flower Show, Pip revealed her long-held secret—her bucket list—a literal list of interesting buckets. In return, her cousins wrote down their secrets.

Home in her cottage with the original cat and the back-up cat, who communicate with her in what she thinks of as Cat-Morse, Pip read the secrets. Jan revealed herself as the novelist Juniper Gin. Lupin's secret was shocking—she had just a few months to live.

After Lupin's passing, Jan met the cats Kittisack and Amberjill and received a bucket Pip had promised her for Lupin's last repose. They discussed the provenance of a family heirloom—two copies of a book called Grandmother's Sunshine. Lacking heirs, Pip had once offered her copy to a young friend, whose mother refused to let her accept it. A call from Jan's daughter prompted Jan to dash off, leaving Pip with Lupin's legacy—an envelope and a pottery cat.

Book Two

Pip received a call from Magda Saxer, announcing herself as Pip's new agent and offering a role in a film called Half-Life of the Lost. The cats were unexpectedly in favour. They suggested Jan's daughter would come to look after them.

Lupin's envelope contained a voucher written in disappearing ink. Pip called the information line, whereupon Gerry Trip, Lupin's ex-colleague at Vouch-Safe, informed her she had one hour to prepare for a mystery Experience.

Gerry's step-grandson, Jamie, promised to cat-sit. He drove Pip to a rendezvous.

Pip boarded the yacht Tulpenmanie, crewed by pleasant Zach, his odd girlfriend, Jisinia, and Jamie's uncle, Tane.

When Pip realised Tane was missing, she called triple zero. Jisinia confiscated the phone but returned it. Pip rationalised that Tane must have returned to shore.

That night, Tane, who was a silversmith, came back. After resizing a ring for her, he invited Pip to meet his family. She agreed.

Tane picked her up and jumped into the sea.

Book Three

Tane took Pip through an underwater gateway to over there where she spent a week with his extended family, practising ballet with Jane and making friends with Tane's spouse, Jillian Jules. The fossmere, a waterfall pool, delighted Pip. She left her tektite ring in the cave behind the falls in gratitude for her adventure. Tane and Jules took her to Hob's Island where she added a new bucket to her list. A sighting of dolphins gave her the idea for a ballet.

Back at Lemonwood Cottage, Pip discovered Jamie, her driver, was a mutie or mutable fay. He had a second self—a dog he called Kakao.

Jan asked if her daughter Clarkia might come to stay at Lemonwood Cottage while Pip had her screen test.

Book Four

Pip met her agent, Magda, at Sydney airport. Magda's friend, Pandora, drove them to a guesthouse run by Edgar and Joan Treadwell. Next morning, Edgar took Pip to a grassy area over there to do her ballet practice.

Pip went with Magda to Diamond Spellman Studio for a screen test where she met the film crew . . . and also Matin Campania, from Arts in Tune, the company co-producing the film.

The filming was to be part of a dance festival. Pip looked forward to researching music for her dolphin ballet.

On the way back from the screen test, Pip visited the Fairy Gardens, where she saw sculpted statues of the founders. She decided to commission the sculptor to make her a bucket. He was away, so Pip left a message with the alarming Frances le Fay.

Pip borrowed an encyclopaedia called Orders of the Fay from Edgar and also ordered a set from Jonquil Orange of *The Orange Grove* bookshop. On a whim, she enquired about Grandmother's Sunshine. Jonquil believed it was a myth but said someone else had asked for it recently. Pip prevaricated, unwilling to admit her family had two copies of such a rare title.

After a return to the fossmere to dance with Jane and work on her dolphin ballet, *Delphine*, Pip went to the Fairy Gardens to finish blocking the ballet. There, she met the Dames with Dogs. Her attempt to use Cat-Morse on the dogs failed. She spotted a mutie . . . a young man with a Scottie dog self. She tried Dog-Morse on an uncooperative black spaniel who was revealed to be Gillan, the mutie's mother. From her time at the fossmere, Pip identified Gillan and her sons as piskies.

Gillan recognised Pip from her role in the cult film The House of Heriot, in which she had starred with Alain Barfleur. Finding Gillan hard work, Pip left, but Gillan made her a remarkable offer.

Book Five

Pip tried and failed to take herself over there without a pilot. She then travelled to Delphinium Island with Magda in Matin Campania's van. Magda asked for details about Grandmother's Sunshine. Matin distracted her, to Pip's relief.

At the island, they met Gillan's son Mull St Ives. Pip and Magda were assigned a cabin. Pip went to the Icehouse market for an official shirt, where she met Jessie and Asher, two elves, and encountered Tane Pendennis from Tulpenmanie and the fossmere.

Pip joined other dancers and musicians to Dance in the Dawn, and saw Matin's wife, Tamzin Campania, playing her fiddle. She did ballet practice with Tane's daughter Jane, who had arrived with her cousin, Jamie's sister Laura. Jane had found principal dancers for Pip's ballet.

Pip met Costas Capricorn who played impromptu music

for her ballet rehearsal.

Filming began for Half-Life of the Lost. Pip met the actors, members of a company called Biblio-Rep, the crew from Diamond Spellman Studio, eccentric wardrobe master, Ward, and Humphry "Humph" Carpenter-Rivers, the playwright, who had invented a new prologue for two people and a horse.

With the prologue in the can, Pip filmed the first scene with Star Calder-Quince, who played comatose Perdita.

During the break, Pip headed to the barn where she met Tamzin again. She was started to see the drawing Tamzin was working on . . . a copy of a picture in Grandmother's Sunshine.

Pip learned that she and Tamzin had known one another twenty-five years before. Tamzin had been her little friend, Angie Blake, who had lived for a while in Pip's hometown in Tasmania. They arranged to meet the next morning to discuss ballet music . . . and Pip hatched a new plan.

Book Six

Pip put her plan for the family heirloom, *Grandmother's Sunshine*, to her cousins, and received a cautious go-ahead on her suggestion that they might have copies made to share. She also talked to the cats about the possibility of bringing home a fay puppy to live at Lemonwood Cottage. To her surprise, the cats were in favour. Pip decided to call her puppy Tektite.

Working hard on her role as Solace in *Half-Life of the Lost*, Pip still found time to attend a rehearsal of her ballet, *Delphine*. She was thrilled at the way it was shaping up under the capable work of the *Forever* troupe, but a wee bit sad that it was now out of her hands. Since her friend Jane was also unable to have much to do with *Delphine*, Pip decided to work on her little cat ballet, *Queen of the Clowder*. Jane came up with a way to fit it into Pip's already crammed schedule. Star Calder-Quince joined the enterprise, and she and Pip grew closer. They were so engrossed in conversation that they almost missed a filming call — twice. Pip's agent, Magda, was angry, and Pip promised to do better.

Star's daughter Candlemas asked to join the cat ballet. Star confided to Pip that the *Caraway's Comforts* brand of skincare was in fact her family's business. Pip wanted to know more, but Star couldn't tell her. It was time they were both onstage.

Book 7, the one you are about to read, begins on Delphinium Island, where filming concludes and Pip encounters another old friend, then moves back to Tasmania where Pip and a new friend share an escapade . . . and pizza.

The story continues . . .

PART ONE. DELPHINIUM ISLAND

April

CHAPTER ONE. PIPPIN PEARMAIN'S ESSENTIALS

Pippin Pearmain had a problem.

It wasn't a big problem in the scheme of things. After all, Pippin was sixty-six years old and, until a couple of weeks ago, she had been unofficially retired from performing for over a decade. Now she had a role in an indie film being made as part of a dance festival on Delphinium Island. It was all down to Magda Saxer's determination to track Pip down at her quiet cottage in Jellico Bay.

It wasn't a *big* problem, but it wounded Pip's ego. For a small, odd, and mostly underestimated woman, pride was an important possession. Pip had been a professional for close to fifty years. Her roles were offbeat and eclectic, but in the business it was said that tiny Pippin Pearmain was utterly professional and totally reliable.

Too A.D.D. or *O.C.D.* or *uptight not to be* was something they usually added, using whatever term was in vogue in 1967 or 1992.

Pip didn't believe she was obsessive or compulsive, and she was certainly not attention deficient. She had no diagnosed disorder, or any disorder indeed. How could she have a disorder when she loved order so much?

She had routines. She loved lists. Since her mother and her lifelong agent had died three days apart in 2012, Pip had assiduously protected her heart from dismay. Her lists helped to keep her focused.

Living in Lemonwood Cottage with cats for company and a garden big enough to grow an industrial-sized crop of German camomile to repurpose into her favourite tea was good. She had her ballet practice — performed at exactly seven o'clock each weekday morning — and her weekly order of tarts from *Jelly-and-Juice*. She had strawberries and cream on Fridays, and her stock of *Caraway's Comforts* soaps and lotions. She'd initially bought these online, since the tiny general store, *Jellico Bay Essentials*, didn't choose to stock them. Waiting for the postal delivery soon became tiresome, so Pip and *Jellico Bay Essentials* had *words* over that choice.

It was Essentials' choice that they did not stock the *Caraway's Comforts* brand. It was Pip's choice that they did. Every day for a calendar month, Pip entered Jellico Bay Essentials and called a cheery good morning to the till jockey *de jure*. She stalked to the Blush Me Beautiful aisle –Mister Essentials had an interesting way with signage — and surveyed the line-up of available lotions with a doubtful eye. *American Spa. Luscious Lips, Honeypie, Smart Hydration.*

Pip stalked back to the till jockey de jure. "Excuse me, Maria, Demi, Bo-Shane, Iphigenia . . . I can't seem to find the *Caraway's Comfort* range. Would you mind . . ."

"I'm sorry, Ms —"

"Miss."

"I'm sorry, Miss . . ."

"Me too. May I speak with your manager?"

After the first seventeen times, Mister Essentials took to hiding in the staff loo as soon as the CCTV showed Pippin's approaching figure.

Pip took to loitering just outside the *staff only* door, doing the crossword.

He had to come out eventually.

She quite frequently stubbed her toe or jammed her finger during this period, the universe's way of informing her that it thought she was behaving badly, but it was absolutely worth it.

On Day Thirty, Mister Essentials wrote up a monthly order for Caraway's Comforts.

To Pip's secret pleasure and vindication, that reluctant order of *one* tub of Caraway's Comforts Housemaid's Hands for his most persistent and annoying customer soon expanded to six. Jellico Bay hadn't had a housemaid in decades, but the stuff worked equally well for the girl from Jellico Gifts and Cards and the man who kept homing pigeons. It smoothed and soothed. It rubbed in well without leaving a greasy residue. It smelled agreeable, as if the housemaid had just come back from a relaxing hour picking flowers and rubbing herbs in the garden.

Soon the range was selling so well that Pip had to ask Mister Essentials to keep her order aside because the shelf tended to be bare when she arrived.

The look in her eye apparently warned him *not* to mention her thirty-day pilgrimage now that she had reverted to her usual once-a-week shopping routine.

When the poster, Agent for the *Caraway's Comfort Range* took up permanent residence in the shop along with Buy Local and Stockist for Jellico Bay Just Jam and Delmsford Minted Cheese, Pip thought her work was done.

After all, she informed the universe, the stuff was good. It worked far better than its competitors. Not that she'd tried them, of course, but the evidence was plainly visible on her peers' faces and hands.

Apart from her Caraway Crusade, Pip also had her bucket-list, an actual list done in green ink, showcasing interesting buckets she had known. She'd had her elderly neighbour, Mister Clancy, with whom she shared garden tips, tea and Bushman's Best Biscuits. She'd had her cousins, safely living at least a couple of hours away — out of touch since her move, but *there* if and when she decided to resume their acquaintance. Juniper and Lupin, they were called, although Juniper preferred to be Jan. She had a gingerish daughter called something floral, and a husband called something generic. Mike or Mac or Mark, Pip thought. Definitely not Oswald Hopplethwaite.

That had been the situation until the middle of February, and Pip had not had a problem with it. If the people of Jellico Bay thought her odd, then she was happy to entertain them. If anyone greeted her, she always smiled and waved back, calling a cheerful *good morning*, even if she couldn't match the greeter to a name.

But now — Mister Clancy was gone from this Earth. So was Cousin Lupin.

Jan and her daughter Clarkia were staying in Pip's cottage, minding the cats and the grumpy lemon tree while Pip, to her secret amazed satisfaction, had a job.

Pip, after a detour to holiday in a place she thought of as fairy land — courtesy of her late Cousin Lupin's legacy to her — was ensconced on Delphinium Island, making a film called *Half-Life of the Lost* under the auspices of her new agent, Magda Saxer.

She was also involved in two ballets — *Delphine*, which she had conceived but which was being produced by the *Forever* Troupe, and *Queen of the Clowder*, which Pip was producing herself with a cheerful bunch of mostly amateur dancers. She was dancing the lead and sharing the project with a handful of people she had never met until that week, and it was all such fun . . .

The problem was — it was too much fun. For the first time ever, going to work seemed less important than creating and discovering, befriending Star and Jane, and reconnecting with Tamzin Campania, whom she'd known first as a little girl twenty-five years before and with whom she'd shared a family heirloom storybook called *Grandmother's Sunshine*. She was actively looking forward to the puppy she was going to meet in a few months' time, an action sanctioned by the cats who shared her life.

At sixty-six, Pip felt she was growing, changing and maybe even blooming, but that was no excuse for behaving like the excitable teenager she had never been. It was no excuse for chattering to Star about ballet and family and skincare when they both should have been on set for filming.

She'd got there just in time for what she thought of as the *demi-pointe scene,* but it had been a near thing, and she wouldn't risk being late again. Her first agent, Sully, had taught her nearly sixty years ago to be responsible. Now was no time for breaking the responsible habits of a lifetime.

"And—*cut!*" Jasper Diamond, the director, said for the third time in an hour. Pip knew that having a static hospital room set for almost the entire film made life easier for the veteran director. Using a ready-made rep company, plus Tiny Pippin Pearmain who appeared courtesy of the *Sullivan Gilbert Agency* and a random musical couple and their horse acquired by chance for the prologue, meant the performers meshed well and could read one another from the familiarity of long practice. Nevertheless, Jasper seemed a little less at ease than Pip would have expected. That might have to do with the maverick playwright, Humphrey Carpenter-Rivers, who had far more influence in the production than scriptwriters usually had.

Diamond turned to the first cameraman, Steward Bellaire, and raised a brow.

Stew stuck his thumb up in reply. "In the can, Jasper."

Pip held her pose, in case a retake was ordered, but Jasper continued, saying, "Break! Break and thank you everyone."

Allirra Diamond, on the documentary camera, backed up for a wide shot, and Pip relaxed.

Star Calder-Quince, playing the comatose Perdita, the nominal star of the tale, sat up in her hospital bed and stretched.

She'd told Pip that her ability to lie absolutely motionless while remaining alert was what had got her the part of the serene, unmoving Perdita.

Pip, on the other hand, had been cast as the mercurial Solace because Humphrey Carpenter-Rivers, of whom she'd never heard until recently, remembered her from her earlier roles and had written the part with her in mind.

Star got out of the bed and stood for a moment in Perdita's gauzy nightgown, orienting herself on the vertical position. She glanced at Pip and beckoned discreetly with her head.

Pip crossed over the stage to stand beside her.

Star was a lot taller, so she sat on one of the set's visitors' chairs to avoid bending, which would have made it obvious she was whispering to Pip. "Everything okay? Need some moral support?"

"Why would I?" Pip could whisper too. She had the additional talent of being able to ventriloquise her words. She'd learned how decades ago when she was cast as nightclub performer Betsy Pine in *Me and Miss Moody* and used it again in *Medium Rare*.

"Thought that agent of yours might be lying in wait to give you another serve of curry for being late," Star responded.

"I doubt it," Pip said. Glancing sideways, she saw Star looking bothered, so she added, "She had her say and I think that's it . . . unless I do it again."

"Bitch," Star muttered.

"She's not a bitch." Pip tried to think how to explain Magda, who had been an artists' and models' agent for an unconscionably long time, but who was fairly new to representing actors and other performers.

Magda looked to be around seventy, but she was very much older than that and had no idea how long her unusually extended lifespan would be. Pip knew that must make her feel uncertain, because continued living meant continually having to make a living. Retirement was probably not an option, as it would bring her peculiarity into public view.

Magda Quest Saxer has been getting the aged pension for how many years?

"She's different," she managed finally.

"That's one way of putting it." But one of Star's more attractive qualities was her essential light-heartedness, and she tossed off her mood with a tilt of her head. "Okay, Pippin, you know your own business. I'm sorry for sticking my bib in and *really* sorry for making you late. I have set my alarm for this afternoon's session, so if you can bear to stick near me I can guarantee we'll both be on time."

"Thanks, but I'll be fine for this afternoon. I have a couple of things to take care of."

That was true, but Pip thought it might sound like a snub, so she added, "I'll catch up with you later, and if I happen to get delayed — *please* call me before Magda has to."

Star grinned and nodded and went to change out of her costume.

Pip left hers on. Since she was wearing bib and brace overalls with a carnation pink shirt, she wouldn't attract too much attention out in the festival — no more than she usually did. Might wipe the makeup off, though, she decided. Solace's ethereal pallor and soft pink cheeks were effective on film, but a wee bit odd out in a bright autumn day.

She cleaned up, put on the shoes she should have had earlier — either Ward the wardrobe master and Jasper the director had both failed to notice or else had thought it was a character quirk she'd invented — and headed out into the sunshine.

CHAPTER TWO. PROPOSITION ONE

Pippin was on a mission.

She had a proposition to put to two very different people. The question was whether to approach them one at a time, which would be inefficient, or both together, which would involve finding them separately and talking one of them into going with her to find the other. That would take time and she must *not* be late for the next filming call.

Since she hadn't seen either of her targets for some time, she decided to play it by ear.

First, she returned to cabin six, where she and Magda were staying for the duration of the Dance in Tune festival. She hoped Magda might be there since she hadn't been on the soundstage during the filming.

She opened the door cautiously, and peered in.

Magda *was* there, seated on one of the single beds with her multicoloured shawl around her and her crystal whiskey tumbler in her hand.

She saw Pip and lifted the tumbler in a deadpan *cheers.* "Filming go okay?" Her voice was neutral.

"In the can," Pip responded equably. She switched on the kettle and laid out her already-beloved festival cup and the caddy of camomile tea she'd brought from home.

Other festivals might give out stickers and pens to their attendees. *Dance in Tune* gave out custom shirts, dresses, albums and beautiful cups.

"I'm not actually drinking," Magda said.

"No." Pip had noted that the tumbler appeared to be

empty.

"Just thinking." Magda put it down. She said, abruptly, "I miss Tork."

Pip had never met Torkel Saxer, but she knew he was Magda's husband, whom she'd married when she was well into what should have been her middle age.

"Ironic, isn't it," Magda mused. "He's pure alpenfee — a bloody fairy man — but he's still a man with socks and a flugel horn he plays at weird hours. He still thinks I'm beautiful. Bloody ridiculous. Him and his whiskey tumbler and its portable kiss to remind me of him when I'm away . . . Husbands!"

Pip said, "I wouldn't know. I never had one."

"What — never?"

"Never."

"A . . . what is it . . . *domestic partner?*"

"No."

"Ever want to?"

Pip shook her head.

"Not gay are you? Mad about mädchens? Cosy with colleens?"

"No." Pip added, "I'm not asexual either. I just never got around to either marrying or cohabiting. No one asked me and I didn't ask anyone."

"Would you have?"

"Maybe. If I'd met someone who fitted." She switched the subject. "Magda, I'm sorry I was late."

Magda glanced at her glass as if at a lifeline. "I'm sorry I tore the strip off you in public. Damned bad manners."

"It won't happen again."

"You bet it won't. I might tear another strip off you if you deserve it, but I'll not do it in public again. It diminished me far more than you."

Pip said nothing. On the whole, she agreed with Magda's summation.

9

"*I* saw the way your co-star looked at me. As if I was an earwig she'd found floating in her milk jug."

"A bit big to strain out without it being obvious," Pip said judiciously.

Magda uttered a crack of laughter.

Pip relaxed. "We're clear on being on time and professional from here on. I wanted to see you regarding something else, actually."

"So?" Magda looked up warily.

"Obviously, you recall my family treasure — *Grandmother's Sunshine.*"

Magda's gaze sharpened. "Obviously. Have you got more photos of it for me? Or of that other book — the *Apple Tree Prince?*"

"Not yet, but I did call my cousins last night to discuss *Grandmother's Sunshine.* I'd promised Jan I wouldn't sell or dispose of my copy without offering it to her first, but Clarkia — Jan's daughter — said it was mine to do with as I liked. That's true, of course, but I wouldn't want to disappoint Jan."

"Did you happen to find out anything new?"

"Not so much *found* out as *reasoned* out. The upshot is, unless the author was sylvan, and long-lived like you, we can be absolutely sure it's out of copyright. Jan and Clarkia and I talked it over, and we decided that if you'd be interested in having facsimile copies of the book, or even just copies of the illustrations for your gallery, then we might be able to get some printed up."

"I could —" Magda broke off. "Sorry. Being pushy again."

"That's okay, but we can handle it. I think I told you Jan is a novelist. She is going to run the questions of print runs past her publishers. It's not their kind of book, but they could tell her some of the practical stuff. They're friendly, and they value her as a commodity. She calls them the Hot Unicorns."

She waited expectantly, wondering what the Hot Unicorn

boys might call Jan.

Magda said, "Has this plan anything to do with what I said to you earlier?"

Pip snapped back to the subject at hand. "As in an olive branch? Not a thing. My cousins and I discussed it last night and you didn't tell me my pedigree until this morning."

"And you didn't consider withholding the offer in consequence?"

"Why would I? I told Jan and Clarkia I would put the proposition to you. It's probably practical and beneficial to us all, anyway. It's a lovely book, and if anything happened to the copies Jan and I have, it would be gone forever. That would be sad. Let's call it our insurance."

"You wouldn't make much out of it," Magda warned. "Colour printing. Limited edition. Pricy to produce, and the market would be small. And you wouldn't own the copyright of the stories, although if you made changes—"

Pip broke in. "We won't make changes and we wouldn't expect to make profits. It's not much like modern children's books. It would just be a little family project."

And another way I can make amends to the family for not supplying a child to carry on the legacy.

"Then thank you, and please thank your cousins. I would be delighted to purchase a facsimile copy, and if I produced some prints—"

"I daresay Jan would like a few," Pip said. "Maybe the Hot Unicorn boys have babies." She made her tea, considering. "At least, Jan calls them boys, but she's sixty-four, so they *might* even have housefuls of teenagers. Or parrots. Or robot donkeys. I'm going out to talk to someone else now, then to have lunch, but I *will* be on set when we're called."

She nodded to Magda and left the cabin, carrying the fragrant tea with her.

The cup was beautifully painted and glazed. The fact that Pip was pretty sure she knew the potter, her friend Jane's beau, Ardal Cornfellow, gave it an added value.

When she took it home, it would have earned a place in her collection of favourite things.

She sipped the tea and turned slowly, scanning the colourful crowd for her next target, Tamzin Campania.

CHAPTER THREE. PROPOSITION TWO

Tamzin, as one of the directors of the *Dance in Tune* festival, could be absolutely anywhere, but as it was lunchtime, she was probably somewhere with her husband and baby daughter, a couple of dogs, and a miniature pony, enjoying some quality family time.

If I can't find her in a reasonable time, I'll need to leave it until this evening, Pip thought. She knew Tamzin would be leading the musicians playing for Dance Down the Dusk, so if filming ended on time, she might be able to have a word with her a few minutes beforehand.

Funny how natural it seemed to think of her as Tamzin now, Pip thought, not for the first time. When they'd known one another before, Tamzin had been five years old and living in Delmsford with her parents under the name of Angie Blake. She'd had several other names since then, which must be complicated.

Or was it? Pip briefly considered all the character names she had used over the decades. She couldn't remember them all, but she ran through those she could, ticking them off on her fingers. *Arabella Junket, Banshee Mary, Betsy Pine, the doppelganger, the Dorothy, Dream Child, the girl in the frame, Hendrika Bruikspeker, Hilaria, Marigold Heriot, Miriam, Myra, the Old Child, Miss Pasternaken, Polly Pickle, the seventeenth fairy, Skipping Lilly, the sleepwalker, Solace, Swan, Tanner, Teacup Beloved, the tree nymph, the unseen leprechaun, Walnut Wednesday, Wednesday Crocker* . . . That was twenty-six, or possibly twenty-five, considering the last two had been alternative names for the same character. Several of them hadn't been *names*, exactly — in the credits they'd come up as descriptions rather than names. Even those who did have names were often more like . . . well, jokes, and a lot of them had single names. Tanner from *Dingo Nights*, for instance. Was that her first name or her last? Since she spent so much of the film alone, she was rarely addressed. How odd. How very odd.

I wonder if Tamzin's names have all felt real to her.

As if her thoughts had conjured her up, Pip spotted Tamzin over by the Icehouse market building with her husband, Matin. Two goats capered around them, but the other animals must be elsewhere. So must their baby daughter, Music. There were several babies at the festival, and it seemed to Pip that they got swapped among the parents, or sometimes gathered in an unofficial creche with a carer they all referred to as Nanny Lu.

For a moment, on first hearing the name, Pip had enchanted herself with the mental picture of the white fay goat, Nanny Lutana, as creche nanny, but even she knew that was going too far. The other Nanny Lu looked like a somewhat wary human, and she bloomed into delight whenever she saw a child or an animal. The animals and children responded like bean tendrils reaching for the sun.

Seeing the couple together, Pip hesitated to intrude, but at that moment, Tamzin stretched up and kissed her husband, before giving him a familiar pat on the rump and turning away. He went into the Icehouse, the giant see-through building where the festival vendors had their stalls and Tamzin headed off towards the area where the Fee Kaffee staff, who controlled the big kitchen, were setting up for the communal alfresco lunch.

Pip hurried towards her.

"Tamzin!"

The young woman turned with a smile and altered course to intercept Pip's trajectory. "Pip! Are you pleased with your ballet?"

Which one? Pip was reasonably sure Tamzin meant *Delphine,* the dolphin ballet Pip had conceived before handing it over to the dancing troupe to animate. Tamzin was one of the musicians developing the score.

"It's looking brilliant," she said with truth.

"And I hear you're doing the cat ballet as well?"

"We are." Pip didn't ask how Tamzin knew, because two members of her extended family were involved in both productions. "We even have a new dancer joining us tomorrow," she said. "Star's daughter."

"I didn't know she had one," Tamzin said.

Pip was surprised until she recalled Tamzin had almost nothing to do with the filming of *Half-Life of the Lost.* She and her husband were both directors of *Dance in Tune,* but Tamzin leaned towards performing while Matin worked on the technical and administrative side.

"She's got more than one kid. The one I've just met is called Candlemas. She's one of the low-caste minions Ward chivvies around. Not even a powder monkey, poor pet."

Tamzin said, "Pip, I have almost no concept of what you just said."

"Star Calder-Quince's daughter. Her name is Candlemas, okay?"

"Got that."

"Ward, the wardrobe master, has minions — underlings — who do make-up for the cast. They're the powder monkeys. *They* have under-minions who sweep up and fetch and carry and hand them stuff. The under-minions are low-caste, and they're usually eyeing the powder monkeys and daydreaming of sneaking charcoal into their powder puffs or saving the day with a well-placed wet wipe."

"Got it."

Pip beamed, pleased. "You always were a bright child."

"Was I? I don't remember."

"But you *do* remember the book *Grandmother's Sunshine*."

Tamzin looked a bit flummoxed at the change of subject. "Ye-es. If you mean the one I'm trying to recreate for Music and Magic."

Now it was Pip's turn to be flummoxed. "Who is Magic?"

Tamzin said, "Our next private production." She grinned as Pip glanced suspiciously at her stomach. "He—or she—is hypothetical as yet, but we don't want to wait *too* long. We're thinking to launch next year, probably in September. But what about the book? I told you, I think, that I tried to get a copy from *The Orange Grove*. Jonquil said she'd never seen it and that I was probably conflating a childhood memory with a series from the nineteen-sixties. I know the kinds of books she means and I'm *sure* I'm not."

"You're not," Pip assured her. She took her phone out of her messenger bag and thumbed it on. Nothing happened.

Dammit. She'd meant to charge it in the first break. So much for undertaking to be more organised. She'd almost fallen at the first fence.

"What's wrong?" Tamzin asked.

"I've got something on my phone to show you, but—"

"You need a charger," Tamzin suggested. "If Matin was here he'd fetch you one, but you still need somewhere to plug it in. Come into the kitchen and I'll see if Tina has something suitable."

Without waiting for Pip to answer, she veered away towards the industrial-sized kitchen.

Pip sidled after her past two girls carrying heaped plates and watched as Tamzin hailed a handsome woman with dark eyes and hair up in a milkmaid braid. She was kneading dough at a large, scrubbed wooden bench. She wore the same outfit as the two younger women they'd just passed. Pip was nearly sure it was a dirndl and that the woman was alpenfee.

Tamzin and the woman exchanged affectionate hugs, then Tamzin indicated Pip. "Pip, this is Martina Qin—Dequan's wife. Tina, this is Pippin Pearmain, who is acting in the film and doing ballet too. She and I are very old friends."

Tina wiped her floury hands and extended one to Pip, who shook.

Before she could start talking, Tamzin said, "Pip has something to show me on her very flat phone. Do you have a charger to fit a—what is it, Pip?"

"My phone," Pip said. She offered it up for inspection.

"A first-generation Pink Princess." Tina snapped her fingers. "I didn't know you could still get those."

"I don't think you can," Pip said.

The young man at the telephone shop hadn't thought so either and he hadn't wanted to find out. Nevertheless, a sale was a sale and he had unearthed a dusty box from somewhere in a Tutankhamun storeroom when Pip insisted.

"I can help you with that, all the same." Tina handed a pink charging cord to Pip. "It belongs to one of my nieces, and she considers it a sentimental antique, but she won't mind if you borrow it." She indicated a power board. "Plug in over there."

"Thanks." Pip knew Tina had conjured the cord, but she didn't say so. She had a feeling it was polite to pretend one hadn't noticed when the fay did something like that. She noticed Tina wore a brooch shaped like a feather and wondered if it was an alpenfee thing. From her observations of Jane's dad Tane and Tane's half-sister Richenda, who was dancing the premier role in *Delphine,* she had gathered the fay seldom wore anything just for decoration.

Tamzin was human, but even she had explained her dolphin pendant as something specific to her and to her husband, who was an elf.

Pip plugged in the phone and finished her tea while she waited for the lightning bolt to change to a wider band of light. She thumbed the phone again and it came on. Slowly, so as not to startle it too much, she entered the gallery and located the photos she wanted.

Tamzin, who had been talking comfortably with Tina, came over when Pip called.

Pip surmised Tina was the woman who had married Tamzin's first love, Dequan, the friendly blond server who made cambric tea especially for her. Tina looked nothing like Tamzin, so Dequan must be a man who didn't have a physical *type*.

She thought briefly of men who liked diminutive women and shook her head.

That ship sailed long ago . . . or never came to port.

"Okay?" Tamzin looked over her shoulder and added *Oh!* in a long exhalation of delight. "You found an online copy of *Grandmother's Sunshine!*"

Pip was gratified by Tamzin's reaction, but also a wee bit bothered.

If only she'd come clean as soon as she saw Tamzin's recreation of an illustration, she wouldn't have to negotiate an ethical minefield now.

I could let her believe I found one and we have to wait for it to arrive . . . I could make sure I send one of the first off the press to her by express.

No. That wouldn't do.

She handed the phone to Tamzin, who flicked through the five pictures Clarkia had snapped for Magda.

"Oh, there's the boy from the castle story!"

"The Education of Tedwin," Pip supplied.

"And the little boys in the water . . ." Her voice trailed off, as if she might be putting two and two together and coming up with five. "Waterfolk! Where on earth did you find it?"

Pip gave in. "I didn't find it. This is the copy I've always had . . . the one I once tried to give to you. Your mum—"

"My mum said no, I expect. I don't remember, but she

would have. She never wanted me to get too attached to material things. She may have known by then that we'd soon be moving on." Tamzin grimaced. "I do remember making a monumental fuss over my pink princess bed. I hadn't had it very long but after we moved, I never saw it again until I stumbled on it recently."

"You found your childhood bed? How? It's not like a lucky penny or a favourite bangle you might misplace."

"Have you ever heard of Project Twenty-Five?" Tamzin asked.

Pip felt a nudge at her memory. "Ye-es," she allowed. "I'm pretty sure it came up when I was looking for your family online. I thought I'd found you, but the details were outdated — they were the ones I had for you twenty-five years ago."

"Project Twenty-Five is an art installation in a gallery in Adelaide," Tamzin explained. "Each room is given over to a reconstituted room from a particular time and place. The bed was in one from the 1990s."

"Someone recreated your old bedroom?"

"Not recreated — reconstituted. My toys and books were there . . . the bed and my clothes from that time. It was surreal."

It certainly sounded so to Pip. "Did you know beforehand?"

"Not exactly. I knew something dodgy was going on, but when Matin and I went to the gallery, I finally found out more or less what. That was just before I ran my parents to earth in a coffee shop and extracted some information from them."

Pip nodded. Tamzin had told her a little of that when they'd met up in the barn.

Tamzin said, "I suppose it's too much to ask if you know where I could get a copy of the book?"

"About that — " Pip, seeing her friend didn't want to talk any more of her peculiar childhood, explained the scenario as she had to Magda. She added, "Aside from the insurance issue, we—or I, and probably the others—believe you deserve to have a copy . . . or two, or three. You loved it just as I do."

Tamzin said, grinning, "I have a friend . . . my foster mother, as it happens. She's a great deal more motherly to me than Adelie is."

Adelie, Pip recalled, was the name Tamzin's mother claimed as her original one. Tamzin didn't know whether it really was.

Tamzin continued, "We clash sometimes, but that's beside the point. We'd do almost anything for one another. *She* has discovered a lovely series of books all bound in green and gold. They're *beautiful*. Works of art—"

"Do you mean *Orders of the Fay*?"

"Yes! You have the set yourself?"

"I borrowed one from someone at the guesthouse we stayed at in Sydney when I went for the film test. Now I have my own set on order from *The Orange Grove*."

"Then picture my foster mother, a very forthright but devious, loving but sharp, lady with a husband and sons who adore her, and adoring daughters in law and babies as well . . ."

Pip nodded. She could easily picture the woman in question. She'd met Gillan St Ives in the Fairy Gardens before she came to Delphinium Island. She was sourcing a pup to come home and live with Pip . . . and for that, Pip was prepared to love her.

Tamzin went on obliviously, "Gillan got her hands on the first edition, which was plain and to the point. Then when the deluxe edition—the gold and green expanded and embellished one—came out, she bought that, too. She bought another set and gave it to me for my birthday. She's given sets to Morgana and Githa, and she's bought sets for their children . . . she just keeps on buying them and giving them to people she loves."

Pip thought ruefully of her own plan to buy two extra sets to give to Jan and Clarkia.

I am so predictable.

"I'm sure you get the picture," Tamzin said. "And that's how I feel regarding *Grandmother's Sunshine.* If you and your family go ahead with this plan, I can see myself as one of your best customers. I'll want one for myself, and one each for Music and Magic . . . and any other baby who decides to come to us. My friend Dahlia has a little girl named Daffodil who loves stories. I'd give one to Gillan, to share with her grand-babies, and one to Matin's sister for her children — oh, and his mum would love it, and Nessa, who is married to Matin's brother. My friend Emily would want one each for her girls . . . I could go on."

And on. And on.

Tamzin held up a finger. "Idea! I don't know how long it would take to get your edition out, but if it could *possibly* be done by July? Or even October?"

"This year? I have no idea."

"I was thinking you could have a preliminary launch at one of our festivals. The July one would be perfect — the theme is Tales in Tune. We could turn it into a light show, with music, or do tableaux, or readings."

Pip quite saw it would be perfect, but would it be possible? And a launch? She didn't know if Jan had launches — she thought probably not, since she wrote under a penname and used a martini glass with a twig of juniper berries as her author picture.

A grand launch seemed a long way from her idea of printing a book for Tamzin and a few for Magda . . . and possibly providing some copies for *The Orange Grove.*

And yet — she turned to look out of the open end of the big kitchen to see the festival goers in their bright shirts. Many of them were carrying instruments or porting children. It would be such a lovely chance to share the Laurel-Pearmain-de-Leon legacy with people who would appreciate its value.

"I'll have to ask . . ." She was interrupted by her phone, which blared its vintage ringtone from Tamzin's hand.

Tamzin passed it over in a hurry.

Pip stabbed hopefully at the green phone symbol, almost dropped the phone, and managed to get it to her ear. "Hello?"

"Pippin Pearmain! You answered your phone! You *are* coming on!"

"I promised you I would."

"I know you did. That was mean of me." Jan sounded uncommonly bouncy, Pip thought.

"Have you been into my medicinal brandy?"

"If you mean that bottle your dad had for his seventieth and which is still hermetically sealed . . . no. I wouldn't dare."

So, Jan has been poking in my cupboards. I told her and Clarkia to make themselves at home and obviously, they have.

"What's up, Juniper Jam Tart?"

"Nowt. I called up the Hot Unicorns as agreed, and they said they've been in talks to open a family-friendly line. Two, in fact. Cool Unicorns for teens and twenties, and Unicorn Foals for kids. They're even looking at Wise Unicorns for the over sixties . . . but I hope they don't. Anyway — "

"Why?" Pip asked.

"Why — oh, because I'm over sixty and I don't need special consideration in my fiction."

"No, I mean, why the children's line?"

"Two of them have partners with bumps," Jan said.

"I see."

"Quite so. Anyway, they suggested bringing out a small edition of *Grandmother's Sunshine* to test the waters. If they can do reasonable sales figures, then they'll look to commissioning new books, and also to bringing out new versions of other forgotten titles . . . sort of newborns and reincarnations, though they won't call them that, I trust."

"When would this be?" Pip thought reincarnated books might be fun.

"As soon as they can scan my copy into the system. *But* I won't go ahead unless you are totally in favour. Oh, and we would have a proper legal agreement. We're not copyright holders, but we *do* own the physical books. They're not obligated to give us anything, but they suggested a tiny royalty or compensatory payment. Or—"

Pip said, "It's fine with me. You know what you're doing. I haven't a clue about publishing, but if there *could* be copies done by July . . ." She told Jan about Tamzin's suggestion.

"Onto it," Jan said. "I agree it would be a wondrous opportunity, so it's all go for the Last of the Laurels! Bye-bye, Pip. I'll put the wheels in motion. Love you!"

She hung up.

Pip, meaning to respond, saw the call disconnect. *Love you?* "But at least she didn't say *toodles*," she said aloud.

"Who says *toodles*?" Tamzin asked.

"A madwoman called Frances le Fay, that's who. She said it when I was trying to commission a woodworker to make me a bucket. Which reminds me. I *have* to find out how to do decoupage." Pip disconnected the borrowed charger and put her phone away, smiling her thanks to Tina, who was again up to her wrists in dough. "Would you like a new copy of a lovely vintage children's book, Tina?" she asked.

Martina looked up and her cheeks, already a healthy pink, turned a shade darker. "How did you—"

"Pip means her family treasure," Tamzin said. "We're hoping to launch it at Tales in Tune, if it can be done in time."

"Ah." Tina nodded. The charger vanished.

Tamzin didn't even blink. She said to Pip, "I take it that was your cousin on the phone, and not the madwoman with the bucket? She sounds excitable."

"It was, and she did. It's odd, because normally she's not."

"I hope it means something wonderful has happened for her," Tamzin said.

"So do I. Anyway, as you may have gathered, she's got her publishers on the hook. No idea of timeframe, but she sounds keen. You *do* know that if it comes off you'll have Hot and Cold Running Unicorns and possibly the Oranges from the bookshop cluttering up your festival? Not to speak of Jan and Clarkia . . . and maybe even Jan's husband, if he's still in the picture."

And if Clarkia comes to Delphinium Island, who will look after the cats . . . oh, Jamie will do it. They'll love to have Kakao to stay.

"That's fine. As long as they sign the *No Harm* declaration."

"I can't see why anyone would have a problem with signing that," Pip said.

Tamzin shrugged. "No sign, no entry. Mull will hex them . . . or something."

That reminded Pip of something. "Star's daughter . . . remember?"

"Um . . . Michaelmas?"

"Candlemas. Evidently she was traumatised by your foster brother on the boom gate."

"I don't see how," Tamzin said. "Unless . . . Oh, he wouldn't have!"

"Turned into a Scottie dog in the blink of an eye?" Pip suggested.

Tamzin laughed. "I do hope not." She sobered. "I can see how that might traumatise an unprepared girl. It's also possible she liked the look of him, then perceived the wedding ring, or even got a *stare* from Morgana. Let me tell you, Pip, you—"

"Don't mess with Morgana."

Tamzin narrowed her eyes. "Pip, my old friend, there's a *lot* more to you than meets the eye. Whatever happens with the books, can we *please* never lose one another again? I have a circle of lovely women who have my back and whose backs

I will always have in return. I don't see some of them very often, but they are *there*. I'd love to add you to my circle . . . if you're up for it."

Absolutely-bally-not. Pip was scandalised at the idea of being a *lovely woman* and attached to *a circle*.

"I'd . . . I'd like that." Pip ducked her head. A nasty thought came to her. "What's the time?"

Tamzin said, "According to Tina's cuckoo clock up there, it's around half-twelve. Why?"

Pip exhaled with relief. She could have some lunch *and* keep her commitment to Magda.

She accompanied Tamzin out of the big kitchen. "I take it Tina's expecting?" she said.

"I have no idea — officially."

"Unofficially?"

Tamzin smiled. "Dequan's been looking super pleased with himself, so I have my unofficial suspicions. I'm not asking, though. People have a right to their secrets."

"Unless they're your parents. Oops — sorry. That slipped out."

"Not to worry. I'm quite aware of my double-think on that subject. I *think* I've worked it out, though. How's this for a philosophy? People have a right to their secrets as long as they're not wilfully hoarding information someone has a moral right to share."

"That sounds reasonable," Pip said. She wondered whether she could stand up on that platform. She added, "And whether your old boyfriend and his wife are having a baby or not isn't information you have a moral right to share."

"Exactly," Tamzin said. She grinned, and added, "Mind you, babies don't stay secret for very long, generally. I should think the next festival might spill the news — if there is any — without anyone having to ask. It would be nice, though."

CHAPTER FOUR. A SHOW, SURELY?

The next few days flowed by like a bright dream.

Pip and Star kept their pact to be on time for work, and Magda thawed unreservedly and regained her apparent pleasure at networking her way around the festival.

Candlemas joined *Queen of the Clowder* and slipped into the role of Downtrodden Tabby as if it had been made for her.

Actually . . . it had. Pip realised Candlemas had inserted herself and the character into the ballet sideways, in a move worthy of Jane Pendennis. In fact, the young women had a lot in common. They were lovely to look at, earnest, sweet-natured, and enthusiastic. They were also as determined as terriers, and shared a useful mix of tunnel vision and lateral thought. Candlemas was evidently fully human, and Jane definitely wasn't, but Pip watched the pair with interest to see what would evolve.

Jane, too, had engineered a plum role for herself. She had decided to be Hopeful, the heir apparent to the old queen, whose place at the top was by no means secured. Jane the fairy with the plain name and Candlemas the human with the unusual one were both beloved daughters blessed with charm and family who saw them kindly but clearly. Pip predicted instant friendship or instant foeship—if that was a word. There seemed no chance of middle ground indifference.

To Pip's relief, it was the former. The girls took to one another and developed a disconcerting way of communicating volumes with a glance or gesture.

Pip turned her enquiring gaze on Laura, who was close companion, beloved cousin and mentor to Jane.

"Do you mind?"

She knew it was none of her business, but conversely, it was, because *Queen of the Clowder* was her business and if Laura and Jane fell out it might affect their on-stage relationship.

Laura chuckled. "Not a bit. To tell the truth, it's restful to have Jane focused on someone else for a change. She's a wee bit full-on, in case you haven't noticed." She glanced at Amaryllis Trip, who was, however improbably, her aunt. "Ammie and I get along beautifully because we're the straightforward ordinary ones. Richenda and Jane are the shooting stars, always going off like a rocket."

Pip opened her mouth to comment, but Laura cut her off. "I'm not being self-denigrating or mean to Ammie. She's beautiful, of course, but we both like to enjoy our lives rather than striving for the stratosphere. Jane's younger than the rest of us, and more . . ." She paused. "Look, Ammie and I have always lived *over here*. Richenda shuttles back and forth. She *lives* at Treborrow, nominally, but her mother is human, so they have close ties here. Jane lives purely at the fossmere."

As usual when people responded to a simple question with floods of intimation, Pip withdrew a bit. "I see. That's good then," she said.

Laura looked a bit startled, then she grinned. "TMI?"

"Not a bit," Pip said politely.

Laura said, "Fibber. Let's take it back a notch. I don't mind that Jane has found a friend on her fervency wavelength. Okay?"

"Okay." Pip nodded.

Once Jane and Candlemas had assigned themselves roles, the rest of the cast quickly followed suit, settling into the personae they wanted to present. The brothers Tempo and Tango

Merriweather, whose younger sibling was one of the stars of the Forever troupe, had become the tommies, lanky boy cats who were feeling the spring and easily distracted. They had inbuilt rhythm and natural comedy and Pip, after the first couple of rehearsals, gave up any idea of directing them and allowed them to work it out themselves. The Dad, Grant Chapman, was Puss in Boots, a solid tomcat with ambitions and a work ethic. Pip watched, fascinated, as he danced classical ballet steps in steel-capped work boots. The things must have weighed a tonne.

"Aren't they heavy?" she ventured during a brief water break.

"Used to them," Grant said. His eyes crinkled. "I'm a welder and I work in heavy construction."

"And you do ballet."

He shrugged. "My kid learned for a while. I used to practise with her. A couple of years was enough—she moved on to tennis, but I'd got the bug, so I joined the Dads."

"Does she still play tennis?"

"Nope. Synchronised swimming. She's good."

Pip visualised a water ballet with synchronised salmon and mentally slapped her fingers.

The rest of her cats were Star Calder-Quince, the deceptively normal-looking Laura Pendennis, and Amaryllis Trip, who submitted themselves as sly Slinky Twinkle, tentative TipToe, and indolent Sit-in-the-sun.

When Allirra Diamond from Diamond Spellman Studios turned up at a rehearsal, Pip initially thought she wanted to join the clowder.

When she suggested it, Allirra shook her white-blonde head. "I'm just an interested spectator . . . Stew's minion. Weird, because he's known me since I was a twinkle in Dad's eye, but he's an okay boss. I suppose you have no objection to me taking some footage for the festival reel?"

"No problem, as long as you don't get flattened by the tommies and Puss in Boots," Pip said.

Allirra glanced indulgently at the handsome Merriweather brothers and the stalwart Dad and said she was fast on her feet.

She was an amiable young woman, and they soon got used to her presence. Costas and Mim, the musicians, even roped her in as Scary Houndie, an athletic but clumsy dog who gatecrashed the clowder's class. That was probably down to Costas, Pip mused. He'd come up with some romping dog music and wanted to use it.

So, *Queen of the Clowder* grew like a snowball rolling down a hill with so many tiny subplots and character interactions that Pip felt quite humbled at the way her vanity piece, as she had thought of it, had developed. Like the clowder it showcased, it worked as a cooperative.

Costas never wrote down his music, which might have been a problem, but on the third day, Star arrived with Humph in tow. As well as being the scriptwriter for *Half-Life of the Lost,* Humph had appointed himself as recorder and transcriber of newly improvised music for anyone who flagged him down. Often, he flagged *himself* down, seeming to have a talent for turning up and inserting himself into proceedings so deftly that no one noticed his input until it was a done deal.

He stood by Costas and Mim, and the flute-playing priest who had wandered in from somewhere and joined the crew, rocking on his toes and beaming as he held his patent recording device aloft. His gold tie-pin twinkled and his quiff bobbed with joie de vivre as he conducted with one hand and recorded with the other.

Until then, Pip hadn't realised they ought to have a conductor.

Amateur, she chided herself, but then she relaxed. Wasn't

Queen all about celebrating the amateur?

At the end of the rehearsal, Humph executed a quite cred-itable soft shoe shuffle, and announced he was Dappercat, the queen's uncle, who had his own clowder and who had come to watch from the sidelines in case there was a likely young princess to appropriate. He would conduct, and he would also dance his turn to show the gentleman cats exactly how it ought to be done.

Pip had no idea if he was serious or not.

Humph was considerably older than Pip, though not closely approaching Magda's century plus. Pip decided that, depending on one's point of view, he was either a fine exam-ple of aging with enthusiasm or an utter nutcase.

With all this packed into a single hour each morning, not long after spending another full hour with *Dancing in the Dawn* Pip thought she wouldn't be surprised at anything. It also occurred to her, in a small alcove of her mind, that, after all this creative activity, balance-boarding between structure and freestyle, being at home in her cottage and doing her practice alone with only the censorious cats for company might be rather . . . flat.

She considered that for a few minutes, picturing her return to the peace and order of her established routine. Clarkia might still be there after her return, although Jan had left the day after her call.

Maybe Clarkia would like to do some ballet?

Her mind wandered to the fossmere, which was her fa-vourite place in the world . . . if it *was* in the world. She was not too sure of that. It would be wonderful if she could visit sometimes, and she knew from Jules that Jane's extended family would welcome her, but the fact was that although mainland Australia had multiple gateways leading to *over there*, none of them was accessible to a full human, or even a trace fay. She'd have to find what Magda termed a *pilot*. That would mean assessing everyone she met for the so-called *markers* of the fay, in the hopes of finding one with the time and inclination to conduct her through the gate and down to the chalklands. Coming back would be all right. The fossmere family would see to her safe return.

Yet even that would be a fruitless occupation once she got home, because apparently the only gateway in the island state of Tasmania was the scary underwater cave through which Tane had taken her on her initial visit *over there*. And that was accessible only by boat and was several hours from shore.

She supposed she *might* hire the part-time crew of *Tulpen-manie* to take her to the underwater gateway, but as only fay with extreme water talent could make the dive and conduct a human safely through, that idea was probably a washout.

No pun intended.

Pip pulled herself up. Moping in advance was not a good idea.

Enjoy your good fortune while it lasts . . . and remember, you might *be back for a book launch sometime this year. And remember, no one* has this life in perpetuity. This is a festival.

Then she thought of the waterfolk and leprechauns *over there* . . . and of Tamzin and Matin who orchestrated four major festivals and several minor ones a year.

After a week of practice, *Queen of the Clowder* seemed fully developed and ready to—what? Pip realised she'd never planned beyond enjoying herself and giving Jane an interim project while she waited to deem herself good enough to apply to join *Forever*. Now it was done . . . and what? Humph had taken down the music and danced himself into his role, and Pip herself had worked up the notation for the choreography. It was no longer an idea, or a bit of fun, or a compensation for less than professional or part-time dancers, but a tight little one-act ballet.

With this in mind, she called a halt to the rehearsal with fifteen minutes remaining.

Everyone seemed surprised but faces turned obediently in her direction.

Pip said, without preamble, "What are we going to do with this?"

They obviously understood what she was asking. Glances were traded. The tommies' dancing gazes, grey with gold flecks, turned to one another and back to Pip.

The dark-eyed priest, who had brought along a broad-hipped young woman to play a lap harp, said in a lilting Welsh accent, "We'll put on a show, surely?"

The enthusiastic chorus of assent might have raised the barn roof had it not been so high.

That simple, Pip thought. They'd made something good between them, and now they were ready to show it to the world . . . or at least to the festival.

"How is that going to happen?" she asked.

Humph said, "Someone should ask Matin or Tamzin. Isn't there something or other we signed that lets us be autonomous?"

"The *no harm* declaration," the priest's companion said. "I think that means we can set up somewhere so long as we're not in anyone's way."

"Quite right, cariad," the priest said. "And if someone does as Humph says and puts it to the directors, a clear space might be found for a performance . . . possibly during communal lunch."

"Fine idea . . . um . . ." Humph waggled his fingers, obviously trying to recall the priest's name.

"Dai," someone said softly.

"Dai . . . Do I know you? Other than *here* I mean?"

"I shouldn't think so," the priest said. "I'd recall if you were one of my flock."

"Where do you preach?"

"Wherever I'm needed . . . otherwise at St Botolphs

Gateway Church."

"Don't know it, but if I ever happen by on a Sunday morning – "

"You'll be welcome."

"Might take you up on it."

Silence fell again, and everyone looked at Pip.

They were waiting for her to decide.

And why not? *Queen of the Clowder* was her ballet.

Pip swept a *grande reverence* to everyone. The others responded, even Humph, with a bouncy little bow.

"I have to be on-set with Star in an hour, but I'll see Tamzin as soon as I can to book our spot in the sun," Pip said.

At that point, Candlemas, who also had to be on-set, cleared her throat. "Miss Pip? Have you thought of costumes?"

What . . . Oh!

The priest's companion said, "Leotards and tights, I should think. Alice bands with ears, braided stocking for tails, and some props for the individual shows . . . top hats for the tommies, and a boa for Slinky. TipToe could have leg warmers, and Hopeful might have a little wreath of flowers. Dappercat . . . a hat and cane? Puss in Boots has his boots already – Grant, want anything else?"

"A hard hat," Grant said.

"That can be done." She turned her gaze on Candlemas. "Downtrodden Tabby could have a dull-coloured wrap skirt that peels off to show a sparkly one when she gets her confidence. Sit-in-the-sun – a little parasol. And the queen will have a crown. Easy peasy."

I'm glad you think so, Pip thought, but Star said, "Ward will have a lot of stuff we can use – I should think we could find most of that in his hampers, though we'll have to make the ears and tails. We have panto stuff for Dick Whittington's cat, but we'll need more sets."

"I can make those," the woman said.

"That's grand," Humph said. He added, "I'm sorry, but who are you again?"

"This is Grace, my wife," Dai the priest said, putting an arm around her.

Humph nodded. "Great, my felicitations on an excellent choice of helpmeet, although I may not remember." He frowned. "Here's hoping I can recognise *my* wife when I get home." He brightened. "If all else fails, if a lady seizes me around the neck and drags me to the bedroom I'll have to hope it's her."

There was a stunned silence, then the priest laughed, and Jane did a sudden twirl. "Mistress Daffyd, do you need some help with the costuming? I can do plain sewing and I remember sizes. Dadda says I have a good eye."

Grace nodded. "We can go to see — " She glanced at Star.

"Ward," Star said. "I'll come with you in case he gets high-hatted."

Pip thought she and Candlemas might as well go too, because they had to be on-set soon anyway.

Allirra said she'd tag along to film the costume scene for the documentary reel. That left Laura, Amaryllis, Grant and the two young men, who said *they* were going to breakfast.

Good call, Pip thought. A detour past the tables was definitely in order.

CHAPTER FIVE. PREMIERE

Q*ueen of the Clowder* premiered as an early matinee. Just as its rehearsals had occupied the blocks of time Pip usually set aside for practice, so its performance occupied the usually idle extended lunch hour.

Allirra had somehow manoeuvred Stew into playing Camera 2 to her Camera 1 and had hauled in her father to take over during her brief iteration as Scary Houndie, which she danced replete with a trailing leash which was briefly commandeered as a skipping rope by the tommies.

Pip was unclear about the filming and exactly why so much was being done, but she didn't ask. She was stuffed to the gills with information already. The festival seemed to be charging along like a juggernaut and she had lost track of what day it was.

Queen brought a storm of applause and much laughter. Pip took her curtain call in a glowing daze of achievement.

For just one enchanted hour, tiny Pippin Pearmain had been a principal dancer, wearing a silver leotard and a silver tiara . . . and it was no piece of stage jewellery. It was made from real silver in a one-of-a-kind design, set with chrysoberyl cat's eye gems and a faceted prism that cast rainbows over the queen as she danced.

Pip had felt her eyes bug when Grace, who had become their unofficial dresser, handed it to her. "Where on —"

"Compliments of *Pisky Waters*, Miss Pip," Grace said. She took back the tiara and set it neatly on Pip's head, where it fitted perfectly into the victory rolls hairstyle Grace had achieved in less time than seemed possible.

Pip, peeping in the mirror Jane held up for her, saw herself not as her wispy, odd little self, but as the beloved queen, not young, but still ruling her clowder with a firm paw.

If only the cats could see me now! Even Kittisack might be impressed.

Then what Grace had said settled into her mind.

Compliments of Pisky Waters. That meant Tane, who was Jane's father, and an altogether unsettling person whose generous helping of waterfolk blood meant he was as at home in water as on land

"Did you ask your dad to do this for me?" she asked Jane.

Jane clasped her hands in her characteristic way, dropping the mirror, which Grace caught out of the air. "Yes, and isn't it *perfect*? Dadda was *so* happy to do it. He *loves* making presents for people he likes."

Pip raised her hands to touch the delicate tiara. She'd told her cousins she wasn't a jewellery person, but here she was, wearing her promise-blank puppy bracelet, now shining black on its silver cord, and also a shimmering crown. She thought of her tektite ring, waiting in its niche at the back of the fossmere for her possible return, and glancingly, of that *other* ring, the one she never did think of squarely, let alone wear.

Not jewellery. Not really.

The thought made her heart hurt with might-have-beens.

She turned her attention to Grace, who was making some slight adjustment to the rolls of hair.

"Grace, are you a fairy?"

The woman's gentle hands stilled. "Why do you ask?"

That's a yes, then, Pip thought. If she wasn't, she'd have said, "huh?"

"I'm making a list," she said.

"Of fairies? There's a delightful set of books—"

"I know. I borrowed them from Edgar at the guesthouse,

and I also ordered them from a bookshop so I can have them at home for my collection. This is a list for myself, though . . . a list of the orders I see at the festival."

"I'm not sure I qualify as any more than a trace fay," Grace said. "You have my husband on your list, I assume?"

"Ye-es, but I'm not sure of his order."

"He's a griff teg from the valleys. There are so many called Dai in those parts that they have extras to their names. They call my Dai *Dai the Voice*. There! Perfect!" She stepped back, and admired her handiwork as she added, "As for me, Mum's human, at least, mostly. Dad's around one third human."

"What's the rest?" Pip enquired.

"It's probably easier to say what *isn't* the rest," Grace said drily. "There's some pisky, a bit of teg, some leprechaun . . . and probably something or other else. Who knows? Well — I assume Dad does, but he's just as likely to tell you his mother was a reindeer. I assure you she isn't. She's a . . . something. *Possibly* human with a dab of delftvolk and some fjordfee. And I love her to bits. So that makes me a packet mix, I guess. Kind of fairy liquid — just add water. Or human, in my case."

Jane said cheerfully, "Oh, good! You're just like me, then!"

Grace looked startled. "I wasn't implying — "

"Being a mixture is fun," Jane said. "You can be what you want, and no one can say it's because you're purely a pisky or whatever and thus programmed to be devious, or courteous, or *green*."

"There is that," Grace allowed. She laughed.

"What's funny?" Pip enquired.

"You know what they say of tegs?"

"No. I haven't got past Volume Three yet. I've just finished herdfee and embarked on hobs. I know some hobs."

One of them belongs to Jane.

Jane recited, "They say tegs are slim and dark, serious, helpful, and are often good singers. They're difficult to live up to."

Grace nodded. "Have you had a look at my husband? He's a copybook example. That they call him *Dai the Voice* suggests he's something special, but you could line him up with a dozen others and he'd need daisies between his toes."

"Huh?" Jane looked from one to the other.

Pip said, "There's a folktale that tells of a lake king whose daughter was sought in marriage by an enterprising human man. The king said the man could have her if he could pick her out of a crowd. A whole flock of doppelgangers popped up, and the man would have failed the test—which was rigged—if the princess hadn't had daisies between her toes. Or something like that."

Jane clasped her hands. "Waterfolk don't have kings, but *what* a glorious scene for a ballet. Miss Pip—can we?"

"There might already be one," Pip said uncertainly. "Or am I thinking of *Peer Gynt*?"

Jane's gaze swivelled to Laura, who was busily attaching tails.

"Heavens, child, I don't know! Ask Gervie. Anyway, let's focus on *Queen*."

Jane nodded resignedly.

Pip nodded back, feeling satisfied. Now she had another two entries for her list and Laura had headed Jane off at the pass—for now.

She'd remembered all that after the premiere as she stood tall between Jane and Candlemas, before taking another bow.

Somebody seized her around the waist and gave her a hoist and a hug.

"Humphrey Carpenter Rivers!" A booming voice cut through the laughter. "Put that woman down!"

Pip, squirming free of Humph's astonished and slackened grasp, regained her footing and faced a tall woman with white hair and a commanding bosom.

Humph stared, eyes large with admiration. "Hello,

glorious being. Do I know you? I *hope* I do."

The woman sighed and turned her sea-blue gaze on Pip. "Sorry for that, luv. He gets a bit excitable. Above himself, as my old mum would have said." She offered her hand, which was elegant with diamonds. "I'm Gwendolyn Carpenter-Rivers. Been married to Humph for fifty years and he *still* gets me confused with Dame Dominque Fortescue. Quite flattering, really. I'm heavier."

She turned and waved her hand under Humph's nose. "See? Boy diamonds. It's me. Your missus." Over her shoulder she said to Pip, "He got a ring made and had a diamond added for each child. Mind you, he wasn't reckoning on the triplets."

Pip smiled politely. No wonder Humph was so happy with life. Even if his prosopagnosia condition made it difficult for him to recognise faces, he *still* had this wise and tolerant woman to love him.

And now *Queen of the Clowder* was done and dusted.

She felt a mix of elation and sadness.

As the cast and audience dispersed for the afternoon activities, three people approached Pip. They were all tall, and two of them were plus-sized in every direction.

She recognised them after a few blinks as the Almaclairs, who owned and ran the Forever Troupe and its associated dancing school in Patterdale.

She knew Gervais, the slim and elegant courtfolk man, the best, because he was the one most involved in staging *Delphine*.

He still reminded her distractingly of her old friend Alain Barfleur, with whom she had worked in the film *The House of Heriot*, and who she had just missed working with in *Pageant Spectacular*. Alain had been fair and kind, patiently reassuring the then teenaged Pippin that she would be perfectly safe on his amazing horse, Varian, as his character, known only as The Highwayman, carried young Marigold Heriot off to hold her hostage in his deserted mansion.

To while away her captivity he played the lute for her and sang, winning far more closeups of her enchanted face than had been originally scheduled in the shooting script.

He'd played for her in the green room, too, as they waited for their scenes.

It had been—Pip paused, seeking the right word. *Enchanting.* It had been an enchanting friendship that had never quite tipped over the edge into romance. It might have, maybe, if she'd been older . . . or even looked her true age.

Gervais Almaclair was far older than Alain had been. Even Court Leopold, the lutist whom Humph had conscripted into his hastily conceived prologue, was older than Alain had been then.

He'd written her a note in green ink to say how sorry he was to have missed her in *Pageant Spectacular* and sent her an odd little gift. It was the second she had received from him. One of the gifts she kept on display and used from time to time when she felt the need of some added beauty in her life. The other almost never crossed her mind. If it did, she'd hum herself into other thoughts.

With her newfound knowledge of the world beyond the standard human, Pip recognised that Alain must be a court-folk man, like Gervais and Court Leopold. *He was a fairy, and I never knew.*

She turned enquiringly to the trio as they advanced. Hamish, the red-haired giant, was grinning at her with exultation, and Flori, clad in a swirling plaid skirt over a blue blouse embroidered with fleurs-de-lys—which should have looked terrible but didn't—smiled and offered a dimpled hand.

"I'm not sure we've been formally introduced, Miss Pearmain, though I've obviously seen you at *Delphine* rehearsals. Anyway, I'm Floribunda Almaclair. Most people call me Flori."

"Pippin. Most people call me Pip," Pip said, lifting her

chin. Flori must be at least 178 cm in her bare feet, but even in her low-heeled court shoes she was considerably shorter than the men.

Still, Pip was the one wearing a custom silver and gemstone crown with fleeting rainbows. Pip was the one who had just danced the lead in a premier ballet.

A very small premier ballet, for which she is humbly grateful to have had the chance.

Pip hastily assured the universe of that.

Flori shook hands briskly. It seemed she was the dedicated spokeswoman for the threesome, so Pip waited for whatever she had to say.

It had better not be patronising.

"Pip, it's such a treat for us to watch a production as audience, pure and simple. Even with *Delphine*, with which Hamish and I are not directly involved, we are familiar with the cast and will always be watching with a critical eye. Your *Queen* is a lovely piece, and one of the best features is that it's scalable. It can be adapted to showcase the party pieces of whoever dances the roles in future. It could also have more roles added or subtracted as need be, depending on the available cast. Only the queen is really set in stone."

"Thanks," Pip said. She was puzzled, and she also had to be on set in fifteen minutes, dressed in Solace's costume instead of the queen's.

"We were hoping you might allow us to use your ballet at Forever," Gervais said.

Pip gave that three seconds' thought. "Why?"

Flori said, "It's difficult to explain without seeming offensive. We don't mean to be."

"I shouldn't think you'd bother to be offensive to me," Pip said frankly. "I don't have any illusions regarding ballet. I don't think the others have, either . . . Jane and Candlemas might be good one day, and Grant—Puss in Boots that is—is a semi-pro with the Dads, but the rest of us are perpetual amateurs . . . oh, maybe not Laura. She's good, I think."

"Laura *is* good," Gervais said. "She just lacks the fire and ambition to be a soloist."

"Too sensible," Flori added, with an affectionate smile. "She wants to teach beginners, and also to have a life with her Caden when she marries him."

"That's interesting, but I do have to go," Pip said. "Can you cut the explanation short and just tell me *why* you want to use a ballet made for the inexperienced, the eclectic and a bunch of life-long amateurs?"

"That's why," Hamish said. He had a strong Scottish-sounding accent, and interesting eyes. Pip knew that odd effect was called *heathering*, and she tried not to stare.

"You want it *because* it's suitable for dancers like us," she said.

"Aye." Hamish leaned forwards and down. "We want our school to offer something for the inexperienced and what you called the lifelong amateurs—"

"Which simply means dancers who dance for the love of it rather than wanting to make it a vocation or a living," Flori said.

"And *Queen of the Clowder* would be ideal, because it allows for them to be part of a show, or a festival, dancing to their strengths," Gervais said.

"Size and body shape are no problem. Age and sex is open. Individuality is celebrated. There's no *corps de ballet* as such, but everyone is a soloist, and the storyline supports it. It could even be danced with multiple casts, so audiences might come two or three times to compare and contrast."

"And if someone is wobbly or has less than perfect elevation or a not-so-good line, then it's simply part of the class and the Queen can correct them or encourage them," Pip said. She gave it another three seconds. "I like that idea."

"Good. We'd like to arrange a date for you and your cast

to demonstrate *Queen of the Clowder* to our current new entry," Gervais said.

"Is there enough time left?" Pip couldn't remember how many days were left of *Dance in Tune,* but she thought it wasn't many.

"No' at the festival—at our studio in Peckerdale-Grene Tower near Patterdale," Hamish said.

Pip thought of her awaiting cottage and the cats.

She said, "I have a pup coming to live with me sometime soon. It won't be for at least a couple of months, though."

"Before then, perhaps?" Flori suggested.

Pip nodded. "If the others can come." As she spoke, she recalled that at least five of the others had associations—or at least relatives—with Forever already. It might be quite simple. "Sorry, but I have to go *now*," she said as Star jogged up, beckoning urgently.

Chapter Six. Something in the Ink

On the heels of *Queen of the Clowder* came the premiere of *Delphine*.

For some reason, Pip had not expected it. She'd assumed *workshopping*, which was what *Forever* were doing with her dolphin ballet, meant . . . well, workshopping!

She received an invitation from Candlemas, who knocked on the door of cabin six just as Pip was cracking *Leprechauns, Piskies and Pixies*. She was very much looking forward to reading this one, as she was acquainted with some pureblood and halfling leprechauns and quite a few piskies. She especially wanted to know why and how the leprechaun gossoons could have green-tinted skin when the colleens didn't. She supposed she might ask Liffey Rosheen, who was teaching Irish dancing classes at the festival, but reading the book would give her plenty of background so she wouldn't be asking the obvious and possibly offending unintentionally.

It had disconcerted her to know the *Orders* series was so popular with readers, but refusing to buy into something good just because it was popular would have been as ridiculous as buying in *because* of it.

She was halfway down her supper tea, pleasurably tired from Dancing Down the Dusk through the sunset, while simultaneously eating a chocolate and coffee *Pas de Deux* tart from the Queen of Tarts stall, when she heard the tentative tapping on the door.

Can't be Magda. She has a key.

Pip grumbled her way off the bed and stuck her head out

of the door.

"Yes?" It wasn't entirely dark outside with so many lanterns and floods, but she had to squint to see who had come to call. "Candlemas?"

Candlemas smiled at her. She had cornflower blue eyes of an unusually deep shade and blonde hair worn in what used to be called a boyish crop.

Pip looked beyond her to see if Star or Jane had come too.

Just before the silence got uncomfortable, Candlemas plunged her hand into a messenger bag disconcertingly like the one Pip used and pulled out an unsealed envelope with a card in it.

Pip stared at it. In the past few weeks she'd been confronted with two other cards. One had been from her late cousin, Lupin de Leon, inviting her to partake in an Experience with the Vouch-Safe company. This she'd done, trading peace and routine in Lemonwood Cottage for a mystery trip by car and yacht and thence through an underwater gateway to *over there.* The second card had been from Gillan St Ives, offering her a fay puppy.

Both experiences had been unsettling though ultimately good, but Pip wasn't sure if she was up to another one.

Candlemas said, "This is for you, Miss Pip."

As if she might have just happened to be holding it?

"Do I want it?" Pip pondered aloud.

"I wanted mine." Candlemas held it a little closer. "Do take it, Miss Pip. I have a few others to deliver."

"Who for?" Pip asked. Candlemas, aside from dancing Downtrodden Tabby in *Queen of the Clowder,* worked as a minion for Ward, the wardrobe master for Biblio-Rep, and, by extension, for the cast of *Half-Life of the Lost.* She had also, by default, become Pip's personal make-up artist, because, unlike the registered powder monkeys Ward had collected, she took direction instead of giving it, had a light touch, and never, *ever* said *We don't use that,* when Pip informed her of what she needed to keep her skin in tune.

There was a good reason for that forbearance, as Pip knew, since Candlemas' mother had admitted to a family connection with Pip's favourite cosmetics . . .

"Flori asked me to do it," Candlemas said. She added, in a gush of feeling, "Isn't she *beautiful*?"

Pip agreed that Flori Almaclair certainly was. She had masses of dark wavy hair, and a magnolia skin with regular features. She also had two fay men in her life, though Pip hadn't even begun to work out their exact relationship to Flori, to one another, and work she evidently enjoyed.

"She's a florist," Candlemas confided.

"Oh? I thought she helped run Forever."

"She does, but Jane says she runs a business called Big Beautiful Blossoms as well as working on the business side of the dance school."

"And how does Jane know that?"

"Jane knows lots of things," Candlemas said.

Jane undoubtedly did.

Pip took the envelope and extracted the card.

"Oh, you got a gold one!" Candlemas said with innocent pleasure. "Mine is blue."

Pip fingered the card's bevelled edge. Her eyebrows went up. Over a long career she'd become well versed in card stock, and this was top of the range, and handmade if she was any judge.

And she noted, it was personalised printing, not hand-penned, inviting Pippin Pearmain, originator and baseline choreographer, to attend the premier of her ballet *Delphine*.

It was to be held in a special extended lunch hour performance.

Pip sighed. She should have known there would be a catch. An *extended* lunch hour would be bound to clash with the last few scenes of *Half-Life of the Lost*. She raised her chin. She *had* to see her ballet, but she wouldn't just overstay her lunchtime visa. That would be unprofessional. She'd ask, politely, if they could begin filming a bit earlier or extend it a bit later. She couldn't ask for the scenes to be reordered, because, as Solace, the independent consciousness of the comatose Perdita, she was in every scene.

Except for the prologue . . . but that's in the can already.

She considered that scene, invented on the fly by Humph, apparently after he spotted Court Leopold and his handsome horse, Artemisia. Instantly, it had come to Humph that Perdita, originally a bride who was in a coma for no stated reason, must obviously have met a horseman, accepted a ride — in her wedding dress, no less! — and fallen just before her tipsy new husband arrived for the official photos.

It was an effective scene, Pip had to admit. Star, playing Perdita, hadn't felt equal to falling from a horse in a scene she'd never heard of and hadn't signed up to do. Pip didn't blame her. Star was a rep actor, not a stunt performer.

It was lucky that Leopold's wife Tansy had agreed to step in — or rather, to fall off — in her place. A bouffant 1960s wedding dress and veil had successfully obscured the difference in age, face and figure.

Star had still been involved in the close-ups, having taken Tansy's place as the fallen bride once she was safely sprawled on the ground, but Pip's first scene had been the original scene one in the hospital room set. That was the one in which Solace first woke or emerged and found her feet in her half-life reality.

She shooed Candlemas away from the door. "Got to go and see Jasper," she said.

Candlemas, as Ward's minion, was familiar with the cast and crew of the film.

Her face lit up. "What a good idea! I'll come too."

Pip couldn't think of a reason why not, so she set off

immediately with Candlemas beside her. She had gone no more than twenty steps before she realised she didn't know where the director was staying. Candlemas didn't know either, but she thought her mother might. Star, when appealed to in her cabin, suggested asking Humph.

Since Humph wouldn't recognise Jasper Diamond if he met him in the street, that seemed futile to Pip, but fortunately they found the ebullient playwright with Allirra and Stew, checking over some rushes at the sound stage. Jasper was there as well.

He looked up with a puzzled air as the accidental delegation arrived. "Is everything all right?"

Star and Candlemas moved up to flank Pip but let her do the talking.

The crew heard her out, and Jasper said, "But that's already been arranged."

What?

He went on, "It seemed pretty obvious that you'd want to watch your ballet, Pippin. Humph wants to be there, too, because he's doing some conducting. We'll extend the break to two and a half hours and catch up what we can by working through afterwards."

Pip opened her mouth to object that that meant she and Star might miss Dancing Down the Dusk but closed it again. One couldn't have everything, after all, and Jasper was already being what she considered unnaturally accommodating for a director.

"Does Pippin's agent know?" Star asked innocently.

Jasper looked even more bewildered. "I suppose so."

"We'd better go and make sure, otherwise she'll be storming up partway through the second act to escort Pip back to the set."

"That's not fair," Pip said.

Star held up both hands. "I know. Sorry. It seemed . . . look, can we just make sure she knows so she isn't left wondering why you haven't reported for work?"

"I expect she'll be watching too," Pip said, but she agreed it would be a good idea to make sure.

As it happened, Magda was in possession of an elegant invitation herself, which she displayed when Pip went to appraise her of the change of schedule.

She said graciously that she looked forward to watching the ballet and managed not to mention anything along the lines of *what you're really here for*. That suited Pip, and they arranged to walk over from the film set with Star, Candlemas, Humph, and his wife Gwen at the appointed time.

As she took what she thought of as a ringside seat for the second impromptu ballet premiere of the *Dance in Tune* festival, Pip hummed happily. She slipped her invitation into her bag and settled back with Magda on one side and the other *Queen of the Clowder* dancers — all but Humph, who had decided to conduct the overture — on the other.

Seeing the *Queen* musicians playing as part of a much larger ensemble seemed odd at first, but Pip was soon caught up in the stirring overture.

The music rose to its flourishing crescendo then segued into the gentle waltz-time tune called *Silk and Circumstance*. Pip had known and loved it for years as the tune Alain Barfleur played for her most often on the set of *The House of Heriot*, but she had only recently learned its title.

The dolphins entered, clad in silvery grey, *jete, jete, jete* in a joyous sequence.

Pip watched the familiar early scenes, the game of porthole tag as the pod explored the sunken ship, and the discovery of a fabulous treasure by Tamberchime, the soloist.

The pod puzzled over it, and Tamberchime volunteered to fetch their friend, Delphine, who lived *up there*, beyond the ceiling of the sea.

Delphine was hesitant about swimming to the depths, but

Tamberchime lent her a magical bracelet.

Pip hardly recognised the principal dancer playing Delphine. Richenda Pendennis was Jane's aunt, and, as a halfling pisky, was inclined to deck herself in silver trinkets so she tinkled and rattled as she walked. To dance Delphine she'd had to remove most of them, so, as Gervais Almaclair had explained, the magic bracelet could be seen and appreciated by the audience.

Like the crown Pip had worn as Queen of the Clowder, the bracelet was obviously made of real heavy silver. Pip wondered if it was more of Tane Pendennis' work. That seemed likely since Richenda was his sister.

Delphine danced with the dolphins and arrayed herself in some of the treasure, admiring her reflection in a looking glass supported by four members of the pod . . .

Suddenly the scene froze as the antagonist, the seafay man whom Pip had dubbed Phileas Tide, appeared and flew into a territorial rage.

Pip was pretty familiar with the ballet up to this point but blocking and rehearsals for the later scenes had frequently clashed with filming, so she leaned forward avidly to watch.

Tide, the seafay man, was a frightening figure, dressed in blue green leotard and tights, with his arms and face painted to match. His hair was dark, and his eyes gleamed in two different colours.

Pip jumped as Jane seized her arm and hugged it in excitement.

"Isn't he *good*?" she asked rapturously.

Someone shushed her, but Pip had to agree. She'd supposed that Corin Peckerdale, Richenda's usual partner, was not as good at his craft as Richenda was, but as Phileas Tide he shone.

Pip watched, mesmerised, as Delphine, the human champion of the dolphins, defended them against Tide's rage.

From antagonism to interest, and on to attraction, the two principals carried the story along, backed by the dolphin corps de ballet.

Delphine took off the jewellery she had appropriated and cast it at her opponent's feet. She accidentally removed the magic bracelet too.

Pip sat up at that. She hadn't written that piece . . . in fact, she'd never thought of the magic bracelet or any mechanism for the human Delphine to be able to swim with the dolphins in their undersea environment. That solution had come from the troupe.

No longer immune to the ocean's pressure and low oxygen, Delphine made her abrupt exit, leaving Tide to appeal to the frightened dolphins.

Where is she?

The reluctant Tamberchime gave up the information . . .

And much good will it do you . . . came from her mate, danced by the youngest brother of the tommies from *Queen of the Clowder*.

Tide pursued Delphine and found her on the sands. He watched her dance with the fiddler crabs, and beckoned her to join him, to talk, to come to terms . . .

That was where Pip's concept of the ballet had ended, but the magic bracelet idea came back into play as he gifted her with a bracelet of glowing shells.

Pip remembered Tamzin telling her that Mariner van der Strand, a seafay man she and Matin knew, had given such a bracelet to his wife.

A final pas de deux, framed by leaping dolphins out in the ocean, ended the ballet, curtain calls were made, director, music producer and lead composer took their bows . . . then it was Pip's turn as the grinning tommies scooped her up and carried her down to the open stage to take her call with the rest.

Afterwards, Pip looked back on that situation with

confused amazement.

Tiny Pippin Pearmain did not *do* being scooped up by handsome young men who smelled of cloves and cinnamon. She did *not* do being hugged by diminutive conductors or patted gently by herdfee men and nuzzled by attendant goats. She didn't do being gabbled at by Jane or bounced at by Candlemas or hugged by Tamzin and her husband, Matin. She certainly didn't do being kissed fore and aft by the excitable Delphine and her seafay man, as a thank-you, so they said, for writing them new and delightful roles.

And yet, that day, she somehow did it all.

Afterwards, she was inclined to blame her golden invitation. Whoever had made that card must have put something in the ink.

Chapter Seven. Solace

H*alf-Life of the Lost* was practically in the can.
Unusually, they had been shooting scenes in order, and now there was just the closer to do.

Oz and Stevo, brother and husband of Perdita, had come together after a long estrangement to decide, once and for all, what might happen with their sister and wife on the sixtieth anniversary of her fall.

It was the *Perdita Unplugged* scene, as Humph liked to call it.

As they convened for the final shoot, Pip and Star took their places in the hospital set.

"Has Jasper told you how to play the post-unplug?" Pip asked quietly. "I need to know, because it will inform what *I* do."

They'd talked of it before but hadn't come to a solid conclusion, because although Humph had implied it would be left up to them, Jasper hadn't confirmed this, and he was the director.

"Not a sausage," Star said. She adjusted her hospital cap. "Not even a hint. I mean, no one's brought in a rose."

"Why would they bring in a rose?"

"When my granny went to glory, the nursing staff put a rose in her hands. It was a beauty — V-S Fair Winds. It's not blue — roses never are — but it's a kind of gentle lavender with a gold heart. The parents are Galleon and Zephyr. I got a cutting and I have it in my garden. My girls have *strict* instructions. If no fresh ones are available, they are to avail themselves of the ones I prepared with Blooms Forever."

"What's that?"

"I don't know, exactly. It came in a bottle. You put the flower you want to preserve stem-first in a glass cylinder, so it's completely encased, then you pour the solution into the cylinder and screw down the lid. When it's preserved, you take out the rose and put it to dry in a cool place, strain the solution and put it back into the bottle for the next time. Obviously, there's a bit less of it, but you can top it up with distilled water a couple of times. At least, you *could*. It worked so well I went to buy some more in case the girls ever got given flowers they wanted to preserve, but no one seemed to know what I was referring to. Of course, I'd chucked out the original box." She brightened. "Anyway, I have three roses done, so that's what the girls are to have put in my hands if Fair Winds isn't in bloom when I die. Strict instructions, as I said."

"I'd want camomile—or marigolds," Pip said. "I could have my coffin packed with camomile tea." It seemed a pleasant idea, although she wondered who would do it for her.

Last Gift maybe . . . they looked after Aunt Helen and Lupin's requests. I should get in touch with them soon just in case I don't make it to my century.

"Have both," Star opined. "And maybe add tulips for your little mum."

"And a lemon."

"And a gooseberry."

For some reason, that made them both crack up, and Jasper gave them an irritated glance. "If you ladies have *quite* finished, might we begin?"

Pip and Star exchanged baffled glances. Jasper was usually the most patient of directors.

He came over and surveyed them, sighing heavily. "I'm sorry. That was uncalled for. It's been a long shoot."

Actually, it hadn't, but Pip thought it must have seemed so to Jasper.

"Have you any directive for us regarding the post-un-plug?" Star asked.

Jasper shrugged. "I had a few ideas blocked out, but Humph insists it's left up to you two."

He sounded as if he thought that not such a good idea.

"We have some thoughts, too, but—" Star frowned. "Would it be possible to film multiples then cut in the one that works best?"

"It might—oh, heck, *now* what?"

Humph had bounced in, with his quiff upstanding. "Idea!" he announced, peering round. "Jasper? Where's Jasper?"

Jasper ran his fingers through his hair. "I'm here. And I'm glad someone has an idea. Speak on. We're all ears."

"I want to top and tail the prologue and the last scene. It'll be tricky, but—we need to have the horse lord back."

Jasper actually went pale.

"S'okay. I've arranged it all," Humph soothed. "We film the last scene part one here, with the plug-pulling, then reconvene to do the on-location reunion as part two in the post unplugging. You, Perdita . . . after the plug's pulled, you will wake up alone in the room here. You'll stretch as if you're just waking from a long nap. You'll swing your legs off the bed, slide down and walk out of the room into sunset light." He turned to Stew. "You . . . er . . . you're Steward, right? You can manage sunset lighting?"

Stew stuck his thumb up.

"Brilliant. Perdita, we want a cross between a sleep-walker's glide and Eve walking into the garden. Got it?"

"You don't ask much," Star said amiably.

"Should be simple enough." He switched his attention to Pip. "As Perdita's leaving into the dazzle, we do a dissolve into Solace, who will enter down on location for her appointment with the horse lord. No worries, I'll have him there, toot-sweet. Already briefed. Got him in especially after I caught him loitering on the cliffs communing with his horse." He beamed around. "Okay?"

Jasper put his face in his hands.

"Let's go then," Humph said.

Stew nodded. "Got ya. Lirry, get sunset themes ready to roll."

Allirra moved to the lighting board, pausing to pat her father on the shoulder. "Chin up, Dad. It'll all be over soon."

Matin came in, looking a bit puzzled. "Humph—"

"Do I know you?"

"Matin Campania. Yes, you do know me. There's a horse lord out by the orchard. Is he yours? He says you told him to be there."

"Yes, apparently we're filming a reunion scene, so the horse will be needed again," Jasper said.

Matin said, "That's fine, then. I'll leave you to it, and ask everyone to steer clear of the orchard at—when?"

"Sunset," Stew said.

"Got it."

Matin went out.

"What do we do with my hair?" Star wanted to know. "Shower cap or not?"

"Not," Ward said before Humph and Jasper could answer. "Darling, once the plug's pulled there's no point in being ultra-hygienic."

Star swung her legs up onto the bed and Candlemas, who had been promoted to set-minion, put the quilt loosely over her. It had to be replaced by the two men playing Oz and Stevo with an anniversary quilt, so she tucked in only the side that showed.

Star closed her eyes.

Pip took up her position by the calendar on the wall.

"Clear?" called one of the minions.

"Clear, one, two, three!"

The set-dressers retreated out of shot.

"Action," Jasper said.

Pip turned the page of the calendar.

"There's a star on today's date. Must mean something special. Can't be our birthday . . . can it?"

She turned to the figure on the bed.

"No? There'd be cards and flowers all over the room if it was. That's if there's anyone left to remember. So many have gone, but we're still here . . ."

She *folded,* disengaging from the camera.

Jasper nodded to the two actors playing Stevo and Oz. They were dressed in baggy cords to give the impression of shrunken bodies, and long-sleeved grandpa shirts to hide their well-muscled arms.

Oz had a walking stick.

Stevo had a quilt over his arm, and a gardenia, which he was trying to fit through his buttonhole.

"Give me that," Oz said, sounding resigned. "You old coot . . ."

Stevo handed it over and took a second bloom out of his pocket. "Got one for her, too."

Oz said, "It's silk." He sounded disapproving.

"Everlasting. So's she."

Stevo bent over to pin the silk flower to Perdita's nightgown. He kissed her cheek. "Happy anniversary, Perdy. I guess this is where I say sixty years married and never a cross word between us—" He paused, one hand straying to his chest. "I don't feel so good."

Pip felt a qualm. She adlibbed her way through Solace's part, but Stevo had a script and he'd just strayed from it. He was meant to petition Oz one more time to turn off the machines keeping his wife alive.

She turned sharply, aware that whether or not the deviation was intentional, Solace could turn the reaction into something natural.

Oz turned to stare at Stevo. That put his back to the camera. He mouthed *it's okay* to Pip and winked, his tired old-man face shifting to the friendly forty-something she knew.

"God!" he exclaimed, rolling his eyes comically at Pip.

Stevo collapsed into the visitor's chair, with the quilt falling to the ground. "Sorry I scared you, mate. I'm just a bit—ow!"

Oz watched him slump. "I'll get someone . . . hold on!"

Oz hurried out of the room, with his walking stick beating an uneven tattoo with his heels before clattering noisily to the floor in the doorway.

"Cut!" snapped Jasper. He turned to Stevo, who stayed slumped for a couple of seconds before sitting upright again. "What the *hell*?"

Stevo shrugged. "Gold script revision this morning. Didn't you guys get one?"

"We did not." Jasper turned slowly to look at Humph.

Humph rocked on his toes. "Must have given it to the wrong person. Thought he looked surprised."

Jasper said, tightly, "Might I ask what is going to happen next?"

"The lads know," Humph said.

"I don't." Star sat up, disarranging the quilt Candlemas had smoothed.

"Improv, kid."

"I'll improv you, Humpty. Better still, I'll get Gwen to do it." Star flopped down.

"Okay. You love Stevo, right?" Humph strolled over to the bed.

"Do I?"

"You do. He's been faithful for sixty years. So, you couldn't have a life with him, but . . ."

Star sat up again. "Got it. Good call, Humph. Brilliant, in fact." She turned to Stew. "Sunset ready to roll? Just after the nurses and things . . ."

"What nurses—"

"Us," three nurses chorused.

Jasper nodded. "It'll fly. Okay, guys. Humph, get off the set. Stevo, get slumping. Solace, comfort him. Nurses and Oz, ready to enter as *soon* as Solace calls it."

Calls what?

Pip took up her position.

"Action."

Pip glided over to the collapsed Stevo. She put her hand on his shoulder, then bent and slid her arms around him.

"Perdy . . ."

"Hush, love. I'm not her, but she'll be with you soon—promise. Just go on ahead and be ready to catch her when she flies."

Stevo sighed. "I always knew—knew you were there. Now I can see you."

"Good man. Right—they're coming, like a flipping herd of elephants. Go now. Go now, before they start in with the protocols. Good luck!"

Stevo sank into the chair.

Pip bent and kissed him. She lifted her head and held a hand above his lips. Then she twirled away and hit the alarm bell.

It was a functional prop and it *blared*.

Cut.

Enter nurses

Exit Oz.

Cut.

Sunset.

The last nurse wheeled out the crash trolley and Oz came back in, looking shocked. He stood over his sister. "Well, he's gone. And you know what, Perdita? It's time for you to go too. I should have done this years ago. That's what Stevo wanted. It would have been better for him, and for me, and probably for you." He stepped over to the machinery, pulled the plug, then walked out.

Silence.

Star opened her eyes. She frowned and sat up, moving a hand to her brow.

"What—" She glanced down at the silk flower, then at the still figure on a gurney.

"Who—"

Pip moved to her side. "Perdita, that's Stevo. Your husband. Too much to explain and too little time. You can choose to stay here. You'd have to do rehab. Most people you knew are gone . . . The world's moved on without you."

Star shook her head. "I can't."

"In that case, you can go to Stevo *now*. Choose, quickly, before they come back."

Star focused on Pip. "You—you've been here all along, keeping me company. I know you. Tell me, what should I do?"

"If it were me, I'd go to him . . . brand new adventure. But that's me. Choose for yourself."

Star smiled. "Yes. I'm choosing. Goodbye, Solace . . ." She settled back on her bed, sighed and stilled.

"Wide shot, camera one. Pull back, camera two," Jasper said quietly. "And—cut! Good job everyone."

Star sat up again. "Are we going to have my bip-machine flatlining?"

"Yes, that can be post-production, though it's a bit cliché." Jasper turned to Humph. "Okay, boss. Are we still doing the horse lord scene, or not?"

"Solace has to leave the room and walk out to the location. She can do the sunset exit we originally planned for Perdita," Humph said. "First, the nurses had better clear the room."

"Gotcha." Jasper turned to Stew. "Okay? *Action.*"

Pip stayed in her corner while nurses hurried in, milled around, replacing the plug and running tests.

Finally, they pulled a sheet over Perdita's face and laid her on a gurney. They wheeled the old couple out.

In the silence, Pip looked around, half frightened.

She expected Jasper to say *cut,* but the scene was still live.

"That — why am I still here?" She faced the camera.

The door opened, letting in a flood of harsh light. A nurse peeped in and closed the door again.

"I should be gone."

Pip came closer into shot. "What am I going to do without her?"

Cut.

Jasper came into the set. "Okay, Pip. We need to get you out of here and out to the location, but we have an hour or so before the sun's low enough. If we do your exit here, we can shoot the sunset scene after you've had a break."

Pip nodded distractedly.

"And — can we change your clothing for the sunset scene?"

"Into what?"

Jasper looked at Ward. "Ideas?"

"Don't look at me, darling."

"Maybe the Icehouse has something," Star said from the sidelines.

"Okay, clear the set."

Jasper cleared himself, Ward and Star out of the way. "Action."

Pip looked around with a puzzled frown. Then she looked down at herself and unclipped one of her overalls' straps. Unclipping the other, she walked out of the door.

Cut.

Chapter Eight. Special Effects

The Icehouse continued to heave with life as vendors and presenters provided necessities and souvenirs. Pip, conscious of how quickly an hour could slip through her fingers at the festival, made her way rapidly through the stalls. She paused for a few seconds to set the alarm function Star had discovered on her phone.

Sunset would be even less forgiving than Magda.

She was looking for Asher and Jessie, the elf couple who had provided her festival dress and shirt on her first day at Dance in Tune. She knew more or less where they should be, but her first stop was at the Pisky Waters jewellery display, where Tane Pendennis perched on his table, swinging his legs, and rapidly twisting silver wire into rings and chains without apparently looking.

Seeing him dressed in jeans and a festival polo shirt still gave Pip a twinge of unease. She had spent a week with him and his family at their home near the fossmere, and in that time he'd rarely worn anything but the odd garment he called a pisky kilt.

She waited for a gap in his stream of customers and onlookers and said, "Still pretending to be human, Master Pendennis?"

He grinned at her without surprise. "I might say the same to you, Miss Pippin Pearmain."

"I *am* human."

"I know. I was just playing with you. I came to watch your ballet."

"Which one?"

"Both of them. Did you get the idea of the dolphin one from seeing dolphins off the chalk cliffs with Jules and me?"

"Yes. And from seeing that seafay man cavorting."

"I thought so. I'll tell Jules. He'll be sorry to have missed it."

"It's going to be danced again, probably lots of times," Pip said.

"Then we'll make sure to see it."

"Did you enjoy seeing Jane in *Queen of the Clowder*?" Pip asked.

Tane laughed. "I didn't see Jane — I saw a young cat determined to take her place among the stars one day. I even forgot she was our Jane, which is a tribute to something or other. The queen is a fine creation — the glue that holds the whole thing together."

"Thank you. We had a lot of fun working it up."

"I know. I could tell." He paused for a few seconds and added, "Janie's been telling me she's going to dance her cat again at Forever with you and the rest of the cast."

"Yes. We've been invited to demonstrate there."

He nodded. "The way I see it, this could go two ways. Either Jane will fall more in love with dancing and we'll lose her to *over here*, or else she'll start longing for the chalklands and decide she can be just as happy dancing at ceilidhs for fun."

Pip said, "I hope you don't blame me for encouraging her in ballet."

"Not even one little bit. Quite the reverse. Richie . . . my sister . . . is dedicated to her dancing, and Jane has always admired her, but you've given her an example of a person with a lifelong love of dance who —" He broke off.

"Who will never be more than passable, but who loves it still," Pip supplied.

"Exactly. So, even if she decides to stay on our side of the gates—"

"*You* don't," Pip said.

Tane's grin flashed out. "I don't, do I? I keep escaping to *terrify the locals,* as my Linda likes to say." He sobered. "But my dad doesn't stay home, either. And yet we both choose to *live* in the place where we were born. We just come here for festivals, or markets, or to visit dear friends or relatives. My brother now . . ."

He paused, and Pip thought he must be referring to his much older half-human brother, Linda's husband, rather than the sons his mother shared with Liam Dancey. "He believed he was human until he was older than Jane is now. It's natural that he and Linda choose to *live human* as they always have. Laura and Jamie too have always *lived human* if you don't count Jamie's penchant for sleeping in a dog basket. I have no idea why he does that."

Pip knew, but she thought it was down to Jamie to explain to his uncle, if and when he chose.

Tane went on, "But as for our Jane—"

"I can't do anything to change her mind," Pip said.

"We wouldn't want you to. You couldn't, anyway. Jane will do what Jane will do. Maybe she'll live with a foot in each world and be entirely comfortable."

"Ardal won't do that," Pip said.

"Ardal." Tane seemed to consider the friendly hob lad who had taught Pip to ride a pony and who was devoted to Jane. He shrugged. "Jillian Jules and I would welcome Ardal into our family with pleasure. He's a fine lad from a fine family, but—Jane will do what Jane will do, and if Ardal wants to do it with her, then he'll have to think of how much he's willing to bend to accommodate that. *She* won't."

"How do you know she won't bend?"

Tane turned the full force of his charm on her, making her skin prickle with awareness. "Because, dear Pip, *I* wouldn't.

To tell me *no* was always counter-productive. Mammy and Dad both told me *no* when I decided to visit through the gates that very first time. I still went. I'm delighted I did, because it gave me my Jillian Jules. Jane is my beloved daughter with twice the charm and three times the will I have, so she *will* do as she wills."

That seemed to be the end of that conversation. It was a somewhat uncomfortable end, so Pip changed the subject. "Thank you for making me the queen's crown. I hope Jane didn't—"

He laughed. "Jane did command it. But it was something I wanted to do."

"How did you come to design it?"

"I didn't. I don't design things. They just come to me. Like this." He held out a silver flower made from intricate twists of silver wire. "This seems to be for you, since my fingers made it while we were talking."

Pip took it and twirled the stem in her fingers. "Thank you! By the way, my promise blank has turned black. That doesn't mean anything bad, does it?"

"Show me."

Pip held out her wrist where the puppy charm Tane's father had made dangled from its silver cord.

"All's well," he said. "It's activated, that's all. There's a strengthening connection between you and the one who is coming."

Pip wanted to know more but she remembered the time. Her hour's grace before filming resumed was growing slimmer with every heartbeat. She was preparing to leave when she remembered Tane's stepdaughter, or *daughter-by-love* as the fay termed it. "Sam and Oash. Did they ever come to the festival? Sam said they might, but I haven't seen them here."

Tane said, "I remember. They discussed it, but they decided to go through to the tower instead. Oash likes to go there for tea and cakes. Another time, maybe, when Soash is older."

"I hope I'll see them again one day."

"Depend on it."

"I have, or will have, a special book for Soash, and for your Mirri and Talien."

"The maids will be delighted. Tally will probably dribble on it."

Someone else claimed Tane's attention, and Pip, still aware of the fleeting of time, hurried on to where Asher Castleby was sorting through shirts and dropping some into a wicker skip.

"What should someone like me wear for meeting someone I knew long ago who changed my life?" she asked.

That had come out tangled, but how *did* one describe Solace's situation in one sentence?

Asher blinked. "Something plain but beautiful," he said.

"Perfect."

He added, "This."

Pip looked at the long slip he'd pulled from the pile. It was plain. The silky material rippled with silver and phantom shades of blue and green.

Asher said, "I think you wear it under a laced-up bodice . . . uh . . ." He dipped into the pile again and pulled out a laced-up vest. Or maybe it was a corset.

Pip *looked* at him. "If you think I'm going to wear that, my lad."

"You should," Jessie said, coming up behind Asher. "It'll look perfect on you."

Pip was about to reply when her phone made a bad-tempered beep.

"That's an alarm, I think," Jessie said.

"Oh." Pip remembered setting it. "I'd better go." She glanced down at the opalescent clothing and gathered it up.

"How much?"

"A credit in the film," Jessie said. She blew Pip a kiss.

"You're on," Pip said.

As Pip left the Icehouse, Star intercepted her. "There you are! That agent of yours —"

"Magda."

"Magda is looking for you."

"I have to be on-set in a few minutes. I'm *not* late."

"I know, but she said she'd meet you there. What's that you've got?"

"Costume," Pip said vaguely.

"Better get into it, then. We'll stop at my cabin on the way."

Pip found herself thrust into a cabin that was the mirror image of number six.

Star gave her fifty seconds to get out of her overalls and shirt and into the slip before she darted in and laced her into the corset. "There — done! Amazing what raising three daughters can achieve. I can even braid hair . . . not that Candlemas has ever given me much practice at that though the other two did, in their time." She surveyed Pip. "You look remarkable. Now, hurry!"

The sky was already streaking with hazy pink and orange clouds when Pip arrived on-set.

Magda was waiting, not tapping her toe with impatience, but looking anxious. "Pip, are you okay with this horse business?"

"I've told you —"

"I know. You do what you do. But are you okay with the horse?"

"*I* wasn't," Star reminded them.

"I've been riding quite a bit, recently," Pip said. "Anyway, I just have to get onto the horse, don't I? Tansy will do whatever riding is needed. I'm not going to have to fall."

"I daresay," Magda said. "But you didn't sign up for

galloping off on horses."

"I didn't sign up at all—you did," Pip reminded. She went on, walking across the grass to where Stew had set up for location filming. Several people had come to watch the final scene, but they were waiting quietly.

Probably afraid they'll be booted out if they make too much noise, Pip thought. Jasper would do it, too.

She came up to Stew and Jasper with Allirra on the documentary camera.

"Okay?" She turned to display her costume.

Stew checked the light. "Grand, Pip. You'll shine."

"Do I need makeup?" She looked around for Candlemas.

Jasper shook his head. "Try it without. This is natural light and you're a being of shine and shadows now."

"Okay. Direction?"

She expected to be given some, but Jasper just pointed to the orchard.

"I want you to move into shot across the front of the trees . . . but not walk. This isn't a stroll in the park."

"Got it."

"The horseman will come out of the trees and pause alongside you, greet you and lift you into the saddle. Okay with that?"

"I am." Pip moved over to her mark.

Jasper said something into his mouthpiece, and some of the minions gestured silence to the crowd who, having stood there quietly, had chosen this moment to start murmuring with anticipation.

"Clear the set!"

Stew looked over to Pip, holding up five fingers before counting her down.

"Action."

Pip started to move, slowly, wonderingly, and now and again giving a little skip. Solace was free of her long vigil.

Now she was going to tell the horseman all was well with Perdita. He'd had a long, anxious wait.

That was her interpretation of it, anyway.

Really, what *was* Humph playing at? In all the films and plays Pip had been in, none had ever been as chaotic as this one . . . and it was all down to Humph's peculiarities. He'd written the script twenty-five years ago and lifted it out of lavender for the joint production. Why did he have to meddle with it now?

Prologues indeed. Horses! It was a *play,* designed to be acted on a stage.

She realised she was humming a tune.

"Silk and Circumstance." Of course. She danced a little.

Come on, horseman.

Ah. On cue, she heard hoofbeats, not galloping, but walking quietly towards her out of the trees.

Someone from the crowd made a long, soft *ohhh,* soon hushed. It could be edited out, so Pip continued.

The horse came to intercept her, and Pip looked up with Solace's quick, birdlike motion.

Her first impression was that someone had spent a *long* time in make-up. Aged from his twenty-eight or so years, Court Leopold's ruffled blond hair was all silver now, and fine lines radiated from his grey eyes.

He wasn't playing in the swashbuckling d'Chevalier costume he'd had on for the prologue, and he'd brought along his lute, strapped over his fine linen shirt.

The horse stopped. The horseman looked down at her, smiling. "So, we meet again, my Pipkin."

Pip inhaled the homely scent of toast. Court, she remembered, smelled of Indian tea. But of course this wasn't Court. "I still have the marigold cup you gave me," she blurted.

"And you use it sometimes. And you still drink camomile tea?"

"What do you think?"

"I think yes. How are we doing this? Humph just told me to be here before sunset. Only I'm pretty sure he thought I was someone else. I've known him for fifty years, though only now and again, but I've never been sure whether he knew me or not."

"He thought you were Court Leopold, who was in the prologue."

"That explains it then."

"And you're supposed to lift me into the saddle."

"Ah. A rerun of *The House of Heriot*."

"I suppose so, but this time you're not abducting me down a ladder."

He put his arms around her. "Trust me, Pipkin?"

"Yes."

Somehow, instead of lifting her into the saddle, he mounted the horse with her in his arms. From Pip's not-so-extensive experience of riding, she thought that shouldn't have been possible. "You're still a little bit of a thing," he said in explanation. "Are you all right?"

Pip nodded.

Alain Barfleur settled her against him. "Let's give them something to talk about—maybe they'll win a golden chalice for special effects."

"Let's!"

He must have touched his heel to Varian, because the horse pranced, reared, and shot into a gallop, hooves thudding for a few seconds before everything went quiet.

CHAPTER NINE. TRICK OF THE LIGHT

"What the blue dickens do you call that?" Jasper Diamond sounded awed but pained.

"Trick of the light," Alain said, crinkling his grey eyes in a friendly smile.

He and Pip were back from their epilogue scene. Alain was holding Varian by the bridle, and Pip was leaning on the horse's shoulder.

Jasper, in a display of temperament Pip hadn't expected even of him, declared that the last shot of the film. If Humph didn't like it, then *Half-Life of the Lost* would go out *sans* prologue and epilogue as originally intended.

He said he felt some kind of condition with a great many initials coming on and he was sure it would reach critical mass if anyone wanted him to direct one more second of that chaotic shoot.

Allirra rolled her eyes. "Dad's having a hissy-fit. How very unprofessional. Who'd have thought it?"

Matin Campania came to try to soothe matters down.

Pip, having caught a reassuring wink from Stew, decided to leave them to it. If she hurried, she might just catch the last twenty minutes of Dance Down the Dusk.

"I have to go," she told Alain, straightening away from Varian's warm shoulder. "Will you be here when I get back? I'll be half an hour at the most . . ."

"I'll come with you."

"Do you dance?"

"Sometimes, with the right partner." He offered his arm.

"Is there somewhere I can put Varian for the duration?"

"Barn," Pip said, stepping away and gesturing to show him the direction. "I'll be over with the dancers."

"Then I'll be with you shortly."

He mounted his horse and rode off towards the barn.

Pip wondered if it was full of goats. Or maybe the mini pony, Hush, or Tamzin's charming riding horse, Ruth, might be there.

Never mind.

Dancing in a long shift and laced vest might be awkward, so maybe it was as well she would not be dancing the full hour.

She stayed on the periphery of the crowd, dancing the familiar steps, with an eye out for Alain. She wouldn't have been surprised if he'd vanished like a sweet memory, but he came out of the dusk and took her hand, drawing her to a stop.

"This is an interesting ensemble," he said, nodding towards the musicians.

"It is," Pip said, raising her voice above the music. "Do you know *Grá Damhsa*?"

He assented.

"Good, because we always have that to finish. It's my favourite."

"That always used to be *Silk and Circumstance,* as I recall."

"I still love that one," she assured him.

"Who doesn't?"

They fell into step, as easily as if they'd danced together for a lifetime.

Too soon, the musicians paused. Tamzin Campania raised her bow. Someone counted down. Humph banged his tuning fork.

"*Go!*"

They were off again, dancing the last seven minutes to the brightest music in the world.

Then it ended. Tamzin, spot-lit now with lamps, lifted her fiddle above her head.

"Thank you, everyone! I hope you'll join me tomorrow to dance in the dawn for the last time."

There were cheers and more groans.

Pip's heart misgave her.

The last time. It's almost over.

It came to her that Asher Castleby hadn't been sorting clothing as she'd assumed. He'd been packing it away.

"So, Pipkin?" Alain smiled, looking down at her. "What happens now?"

Pip blinked. "I expect we'd better go to supper."

They headed off to where the servers were laying out platters in the floodlit area next to the great kitchen. Without discussion, Pip piled an assortment of food onto one of the spare platters and appropriated her usual cambric tea.

"We can go to the barn," she said. "I'll just call at the cabin first for my cup. Oh — you'll need one . . ."

"I'm sure there's a spare somewhere," Alain said. He flagged down one of the dirndl girls. "Mädchen, have you a spare cup for me? I'm late to the party."

The girl turned as if to search the area, then whirled back with a plain blue cup in her hand.

She conjured that.

"It's totally mine to lend you," she said, widening her eyes.

"Thank you," Alain said, accepting it gravely. He took the platter from Pip and left her to carry the teapot. So laden, they headed for the barn, pausing at cabin six on the way as Pip had proposed. Alain waited courteously outside while she fetched her festival cup. She wished it had been the marigold one he'd given her long ago, but that was back at home in Lemonwood Cottage.

Three goats were in the barn, chewing hay in their beard-waggling fashion. Two of them were Nanny Lutana and the one Costas Capricorn had dubbed Uncle Evilbeard. The third was a roan nanny with blue eyes. Ruth, the quiet grey mare, was asleep with one hoof tilted up. Varian nickered a greeting as they entered.

Alain whistled to him and handed him an apple. "There, my old friend . . ."

Pip sat down on the bale of hay where she'd first seen Tamzin sketching.

"He must be a *very* old friend . . . if that's really the Varian I remember," she said.

Alain poured tea for her, and for himself.

"He's—" He hesitated, glancing at her sideways.

"I suppose he's a fay horse," Pip said.

"Ye-es."

"You don't sound very sure."

He laughed. "Oh, I'm sure of what I know. I'm just not sure of what *you* know."

"I've had disclosure, if that's what you mean," Pip said grandly.

"That makes life easier. I suppose it would be difficult *not* to have had it if you come to many of these festivals. At least half those musicians were from my side of the gates." He gave her another sideways glance as if to judge whether she knew the term.

"This is my first *Arts in Tune* festival, but a couple of weeks ago I spent a few days *over there* at a place called the fossmere. Do you know it?"

"Not offhand."

"It's not far from the chalklands and a place called Hob's Island."

He shook his head. "Not my area at all. I'm from Île de lin—Flaxen Isle."

"Ja. *Und?*"

Alain chuckled. "Oh, so you still do that, Pipkin?"

"When it's appropriate."

"Hmm. Flaxen Isle is a far-distant outpost of the Charm Lines."

"I don't know that place."

"How should you?" He handed her a bunch of grapes. "Did you know there's a gateway near here?"

"Yes." She was on sure ground. "I used it to go to the foss-mere to dance with Jane when I was staying in Sydney. I think Edgar called it the castle bridge gate." She didn't add that she'd tried to access it by herself and ended up in a human-side courtyard having a surreal discussion with a human gardener and a large and ill-mannered fay tomcat.

"Not that one, *l'ami de mon coeur*. The one I used is altogether more perilous. Fortunately, I have an old acquaintance — or rather, the grandson of one — who lent me his assistance. His beloved, a most original person, gave me her advice, which was mainly to gird my loins and get it done."

"It's not the underwater one in Bass Strait, is it?" Pip asked.

"No — I don't know that one. Is it close to shore?"

"It's out in the middle of the strait. To use it you have to jump off a yacht, get given water gift by someone with lots of water blood, and hope for the best."

"That sounds unnerving."

Pip considered. "It was, but — do you know Tane Pendennis?"

"I have not that honour."

"I wouldn't call it an honour. He's a pisky-waterfolk halfling, and he has what he calls *love bubbles*."

Alain put down the marigold tart he was eating and stared at her with lurking amusement. "Ah. One of *those*."

"Yes. He says he likes me a *lot*. So does his wife, who is sometimes his husband. And his eldest daughter is one of my dancing friends."

"And you like him a lot?"

"I do. He improved on acquaintance. He's fun. Apparently

he propositions almost everyone, but he didn't with me." She paused a beat and added, "His mother did, though. At least, I think so."

Alain bit the tart. "I see you still have your comic timing."

"I see *you* still have your lute."

"It's part of who I am."

Pip said, "If your gateway isn't one of those two, which is it?"

"Hm." He looked off sideways.

"Don't prevaricate."

"I wasn't. I was wondering how to put it, so it sounds even halfway plausible."

Pip said, "Why do you all look the same?"

"The same as whom?"

"The others. Courtfolk people. It says in *Orders of the Fay* that you keep marrying one another, but Jane said — I think it was her — that you don't always. Flori Almaclair is human, and Tansy Leopold is a hob. Even Piers le Fay is married to a human, I think — he's the author."

Alain looked taken aback.

Pip thought maybe she had gabbled on a bit. "I mean, three courtfolk men I know, or sort of know, have wives, or lady companions, or whatever Flori is, who aren't courtfolk."

He said, "I expect it's just what folk say. I don't know the others you mentioned. Do I really look like them?"

"Older, of course. And when I knew you before you were younger. Court Leopold is twenty-eight or so, and Gervie is forty-something. They're so alike I thought they were related, but they're not. You look like them, only nicer."

He laughed. "Thank you. I think. Why am I nicer?"

"Less pleased with yourself. Not smug."

"I'm glad to hear it. If courtfolk have an underlying failing it's a tendency to be smug or at the very least to be self-assured. To return to the gateway, it's right here on this island.

It's not much used, for obvious reasons. Obvious from both sides, I would think. On my side, it's like this."

He leaned forward and pulled grapes off a bunch, scattering them on the hay. One of the goats stepped forwards with an avid expression, and Alain said, "Later, friend." He indicated the grapes. "These are the Charm Lines, Pipkin. Not to scale, and not accurate, but you see—small islands and islets. Not inhabited on the whole, but they're close enough that you can always see at least one of them from any other. Over there—" He bowled an orange beyond the grapes. "That's my Île de lin. It comes up close to the mainland of Pays des Cygnes—Swanland if you like." He gestured to the side. "The Charm Lines come in to a rocky place where a galleon—do you know them?"

Pip nodded. "Frances le Fay said Xavier Partridge was off on a galleon. I want him to make me a bucket."

"Of course you do. The galleon, *Delphinium*, breached there many years ago, effectively stranding her crew *over here*. They lived for a time as gatekeepers, but the gate was used so infrequently the last of them, Mistress Ondine, has returned to the galleonfee life. Or so my old friend's grandson informed me. What he actually said was a bit more to the point. He said I'd have to negotiate with her tenants if I wanted to go on using the gate. I was on my way to do that when I realised there was something going on down here on the island. I was considering my options when I encountered my very old friend Humph, who commanded my presence for a film. I was a bit startled, to say the least, but I went to the orchard, where I chanced upon an elf man called Matin Campania who explained a bit more coherently than Humph had. Humph, by the way, had gone off somewhere in a hurry."

"The gateway," Pip reminded. She thought she could detangle Humph and Matin's input later if she felt it necessary.

"Indeed. To access that gateway, I had to bring Varian

across the Charms, and up a highly perilous cliff path, which was where my alarming young friend and his lady came in. Once at the top of the cliff, through we came. It's not a route I care to use too often. It's been a while, and I'd forgotten how uncertain the footing is."

Pip said, "Varian. He's a fay horse, and — he must be something else, because I live with two fay cats, and Kittisack told me he won't live forever. He's at least eleven, and he seems to think he has a while yet, but — "

"Fay cats have a span longer than the cats bred this side of the gates," Alain said. "But you're right in a way. Varian is a *cheval du chevalier de lin.*"

"I don't speak French," Pip remarked.

"Neither do I. He's a . . . Flaxen knight's steed. He was foaled the day I was born, and we are linked. We grew together, we thrive together, and together we'll go to glory. I daresay that sounds odd to you."

"It sounds *wonderful* to me. I have occasionally wondered where you were, and if you were happy . . . and I hoped Varian might be getting apples from Little Mum in glory. Knowing he's still with you is even better." She paused. "Where have you been all this time?"

"At home on Flaxen Isle, mainly."

"You don't act anymore?"

"I never officially retired. It was Humph who got me into acting, you know. He was looking for someone to play the Highwayman in *The House of Heriot* and he saw me with Varian and attached us — is that the term?"

Pip assented.

"He attached us to the film. It was fun. I especially enjoyed my time with you, Pipkin."

"How did Humph get mixed up with *The House of Heriot?* The author was a woman — Henrietta something. Henrietta Riviere."

"That was Humph, using a made-up name. He always enjoyed a bit of flim-flam. It wasn't until I'd agreed to be his highwayman that I found out I should have had all sorts of papers. I did get what I needed eventually, with a bit of help from a couple of other fay who were in the business, and I was in a few other productions. I always hoped to work with you again."

"We almost did work together in *Pageant Spectacular.* You left the day before I arrived. You even wrote me a note."

"So I did. You never replied."

"I did reply. My letter came back *Unknown at this address.*"

He frowned. "That's odd—"

Pip opened her messenger bag and extracted an envelope. "See?" She passed it to Alain.

He exhaled. "You kept it all this time?"

She shrugged. "I'm a packrat. You should see the boxes and crates of stuff I have at home. I left the furniture, but I packed up lots of other stuff when I moved house ten years ago. I haven't got around to unpacking it yet."

"Are you ever going to?"

"Yes. One day soon."

He examined the envelope. "You sent this to my agent."

"That's the usual thing when you don't know an address. You'd described your home, but you never actively told me *where* it was, or how to get in touch with you."

"No."

"We discussed me visiting you, but we never specified how that would happen."

"You were so young," Alain said.

"Sixteen."

"So young," he repeated.

"But you wrote me a letter."

"I did."

"With no address, other than Barfleur Manor. And so that's

where I sent it, care of your agent."

"And unfortunately, that explains it. He and I had a falling out after *Pageant Spectacular*. I wanted to wait to see you, but *he* made me trek off to another film-set . . . only to find they didn't actually need me for six weeks. That was that. I came back. You'd gone." He turned out his hands. "If I hadn't been so very green I'd have found a way, perhaps, but as it was, I did the film in question because I was under contract. Then I tore up my contract with him and went home. Now and again I've come through to do equestrian displays or pageants with Varian, and hoped you might be there, but mostly I stay on my estate. In fact, since Mistress Ondine Delphinium has returned to her ancestral calling, I have lost my *lieu de contact*, unless the current tenants agree to stand for me. That's one reason I'm here. Mistress Ondine . . ." He trailed off, and Pip was glad.

It was all too complicated. She held out her hand for the letter and he gave it to her, still unopened. She replaced it, although she didn't really know why, poked her fingers into the lining of the bag and drew out the pouch that had once held her tektite Heaven and Earth ring. "You put this in the letter you left for me." She opened the pouch and unwrapped the wisp of soft cloth it contained.

For the first time in decades, she looked properly at the second gift Alain had given her. It tugged at her heart and puzzled her mind as it had all those years ago.

He smiled. "So I did. It was — call it a whim. You've never used it."

Pip ran her fingers around the braided circlet made of gold and silver threads. "I never knew quite what it was. A ring, obviously, but I've never seen anything like it . . . except in a Victorian mourning brooch in that *Missus Horatia Justice* painting. And I shouldn't think you'd have sent me anything like that."

"I wouldn't. It's a *bague de gentilesse,* a ring of kindness. It lets good friends keep in touch," he said.

"It's horse hair?"

"Partly. Slip it on your finger. I promise it won't hurt."

Pip slid the ring on her finger and felt a rush of happiness. "I wish I'd known."

"So do I. But at least you do use the marigold cup sometimes."

"I do, but how did you know?"

He hesitated again. "I'm afraid I put a tiny charm to it."

Pip *felt* his embarrassment through the link and raised her chin to give him a good hard stare. "Ja. *Und?*"

Alain started to laugh.

Pip kept sober for as long as she could, but soon she joined in. It was impossible not to. Her eyes watered and she raised her arm to mop them.

Alain handed her a soft cloth and, just before she dried her eyes she saw the sweet young man she'd known all those years ago. She blinked, and he was silver haired again.

Must be a trick of the light.

CHAPTER TEN. AM I DOING THIS?

"What?" Alain picked up his marigold tart, continuing to look at her.

"What do you mean, *what?*"

"You're blushing."

Pip put her hands over her cheeks. "I was thinking of my agent—Magda Saxer."

"The fierce alpmaid with the charmed shawl?"

"That's her, but she's not an alpmaid. Not really. She's mostly human, she thinks."

"I wouldn't like to contradict a fierce alpmaid," he said.

"Neither would I. Especially since she's my agent. She thinks she must have some sylvan blood too because she's much older than she looks."

"I see. But what were you thinking about her to make you blush? Did she proposition you as well?"

"No. *What* an idea. It's just that she has a crystal whiskey tumbler her husband gave her. It's charmed with a kiss."

Alain said, "Was he a romantic young tal when he gave it to her?"

"No. Well, he might be romantic, but not *young,* exactly." Pip knew from her reading that *tal* was the name given to al-penfee males. "But my cup doesn't have *that* sort of kiss. I think I'd have noticed."

"No indeed. It was a kiss of friendship."

"I thought so. Using my marigold cup always makes me feel happy—or maybe I use it when I *am* feeling happy."

"I know. It's a two-way charm."

"Long distance surveillance." Pip wondered whether to be offended or creeped out and decided it was much too late for that.

"It doesn't tell me what you're doing or what you're thinking," he said gently. "That would be wrong and intrusive and impossible anyway. It just lets me know that you're using the cup . . . and being happy . . . especially when I'm drinking tea myself."

"I usually am happy when I'm drinking tea . . . and I never use that cup for lemon juice from the ferocious lemon tree."

"So I should hope. It might dissolve the porcelain. Er— what ferocious lemon tree?"

"I'll tell you sometime."

The roan goat bleated, and Alain said, "Go ahead, friends."

The grapes he'd scattered as islands vanished in seconds.

Varian gave Pip a nudge.

She reached up to stroke his soft muzzle. "I suppose it was *your* hair your master appropriated to make my ring of kindness, Varian."

"It was, but I'm not his master. We're more like lifelong friends. Good companions. I might as well cover myself with more confusion by telling you the gold threads are my own hair, as it was then, and the silvery ones are a wee few of yours. If you recall, the Highwayman's cloak was made of cotton velvet, and when you leaned your head against his shoulder, you dropped a few. No more than anyone would, of course."

Pip lobbed a grape at him, missed, and watched the goats dive for it. She scattered a few more for fairness and gave one to Varian.

She sat feeling ridiculously happy and a little melancholy at the same time.

"The lemon tree?" he prompted.

"Oh!" Pip laughed. "It grows in my garden near a

gooseberry bush. They both give me the evil eye when I go down to grab a lemon for my morning drink. They egg one another on. I didn't plant them, and they were both mature when I moved into my cottage. I'm sure they're both out to get me, but it's not serious, you know?"

"You enjoy the battle?"

"I never really thought of it, but I *do*. A victory is a victory, even if it's over an ill-intentioned lemon."

Alain shook his head. "I've met a few odd things in my time, but I don't think I've ever been savaged by a fruit tree."

Pip drained her tea. "This is my festival cup," she said, displaying it. "I'm going to add it to my collection. It can be my second favourite, after my marigold kiss cup. Do you know anything about buckets, Alain?"

"I have them for my wells, and there's a nice one I carved from a fallen tree. I have candlesticks and a chair from that tree . . . and a table. The wood was too beautiful to burn."

A bucket from a fallen tree.

Pip flashed on the Clancy bucket, which she'd given to Jan. That had been the epitome of buckets in her mind until she'd spotted the one in Iris' wishing well on Hob's Island. She remembered thinking the one at the well must have been made from a single solid piece of wood.

It was tempting to mine for more information, but instead, she got up and did a ballet stretch.

She'd love to stay there all night, talking, catching up, eating tarts and just looking into that wistfully remembered face.

He'd changed with the passage of fifty years. Everyone did . . . even the comatose Perdita. Pip was glad she'd seen him older. They were near contemporaries again, after decades of increasing distance. He'd become just what she might have hoped and expected.

Better leave before I do or say something to spoil this perfect reunion.

He looked up at her then got to his feet, tilting his head

with an enquiring expression.

"Are you going to sit down again, or is this a preparatory stretch before you fly away from me?"

Pip looked him squarely in the face. "Alain, I'm so glad I found you again. I've never forgotten you and it's down to you that I have such lovely memories of *The House of Heriot.*"

"But?"

"No buts—just logistics. I wish we could stay in touch, the way we wanted before, but I live in Tasmania. We don't have gates there, apparently . . . or only the one in the sea. And *you* live on . . . what . . . Flaxen Isle. It sounds a lovely place, but I don't suppose you have phones. They don't at the fossmere."

Alain put out his hand. "Pipkin, will you come to Flaxen Isle?"

"I don't know. I wish I could, but it sounds difficult to get to, even from here."

"A message to my young friend and his formidable maid will bring me to fetch you from the gate. Any time."

She hesitated.

"You really should meet them. Life is not complete until you've seen a seafay man fleeing from an avenging beauty who is the love of his life. It shouts *righteous terror* and hums with anticipation of being caught."

Pip flashed on the couple she'd seen at the chalk cliffs. The seafay man had certainly not been fleeing. But then, his lady was courtfolk so maybe she had neither the skill nor the will to pursue him.

"No?"

She said, slowly, "I *might* be here again in July . . . or possibly October, for a book launch. Then, maybe—"

Am I doing this?

He opened his arms, stepped forwards and gave her a friendly hug. "Please come, dear Pipkin. I'd love to show you my world and to see you in it. I always meant to do that. You could stay for a day or a week or a month or so and come back as often as you like. There's plenty of room."

"Do you have ponies?" she asked into his chest. It wasn't entirely what she wanted to ask. A week was too little time. A month or so might be too long.

She didn't do hugging . . . but maybe she did.

"No ponies, but I have a small mare. She's Varian's great-great-and-then-some granddaughter. Name of Lovely. And yes, I named her. My granddaughter used to ride her, but now she's wed and much too busy rearing what my grandson-by-love is pleased to call her *pledges of affection*. Five so far!"

Pip said, "You have a granddaughter! What's her name?"

"Nathalie. And before you ask, her parents named her."

"I'm glad you had children," Pip said awkwardly.

"Just one — my son." He cleared his throat. "To be clear, his mama — Mistress Olympe Arden — and I chose to make him, but we did not choose to wed. We have a good deal too much respect for one another and for ourselves to do that. We deal very well as friends, and we see one another now and again. We spent much more time together when Ghislain was younger. He is our enfant héritier . . . heir by arrangement. It's a fairly common undertaking among Flaxen Isle families."

Pip thought of Mama Tam and the four men she'd chosen to father her bouquet of children. She'd married the fourth one but only, Pip seemed to recall, because he wouldn't give her a baby until she did.

She had met Tam's four sons, and she knew Tane was very fond of his little sisters, whose fathers were a hob man and a treefolk clan master.

She was drawing breath to answer Alain, to say *yes*, she'd come to Flaxen Isle, when voices sounded beyond the soft light of the barn and Matin and Tamzin Campania walked in.

"There you are, Pip!" Tamzin said cheerfully. "Time got away from me, but will you let me do the sketches and start to paint you now? There won't be time to start anything new tomorrow."

Pip's head spun. It felt so late, but she supposed it was around seven o'clock.

That's right. I promised to sit for her.

"In here?" She moved away from Alain's slackened arms.

Matin glanced at her, and she felt obliged to say, "Tamzin, Matin, this is my old friend Alain Barfleur. We were in a film together years ago."

"And in another one just now," Alain said.

"We were catching up," Pip continued. She turned formal. "Alain, these are Tamzin and Matin Campania—they're the directors of Arts in Tune."

Matin said to Tamzin, "This is the courtfolk man Humph appropriated for his mad epilogue—I hope it wasn't too awkward, master? I suspect he thought you were Court Leopold, who is a friend of ours, and who worked in the prologue of the film."

That's right, Pip thought. Matin and Alain have already met. She felt foolish for introducing them in such a ridiculous fashion.

"I knew Humph a long time ago," Alain said. "He was an enfant terrible of stage and screen when we met."

"He still is," Tamzin muttered.

"You may be right, though. He might not have recognised me this time. He has a problem with faces, and I expect a man with a horse is a man with a horse—to him. I think he did address me as *Court,* but I thought he was just being cheeky. He used to call me *the courtier,* back in the day." He reached out and offered his hand to Tamzin. "Greet you, Mistress Campania. From what I've seen in the brief time since I came over, everything seems to be humming."

"We're pleased with the way it's going," Matin said.

Tamzin looked at Pip. "Pip? Painting?"

"Oh—yes. How do you want me?"

"Just as you are."

Tamzin sat down on the hay bale where Alain had been and began to sketch.

Alain said, "Master Campania, I have a request to put to you. I used to deal with Mistress Ondine ... who gave me messages—"

The men walked out, leaving Tamzin and Pip alone.

Pip felt suddenly and extremely tired and mildly woeful and marginally dismissed. "Do you mind if I sit down?"

"Not a bit," Tamzin said.

Pip arranged herself on another bale of hay, humping her knees and wrapping her arms around them.

Tamzin, charcoal to paper, paused. "You look melancholy. I hope Matin and I didn't interrupt anything special just now."

CHAPTER ELEVEN. DEGREES OF FRIEND-SHIP

Pip said, too quickly, "Why would you think that?"

"You and Master Barfleur —"

If she says something coy on the lines of looked cosy together *or* seemed to be having a moment, *then I'll probably scream.*

Tamzin continued. "You're old friends?"

Pip relaxed.

"The way I am with Dequan?"

"How do you mean?"

"I mean, I'm happy in his company. We're always pleased to see one another, but if I don't see him for several weeks — and usually I don't — then it doesn't make me sad."

"It wouldn't. You've got Matin."

"As you say, I've got Matin, and Music, and all of this — and one day, not too far away, I'll have Magic to love as well. But Dequan and I are old friends, and I wouldn't like not to have him in my life."

Pip said, "I'm not sure what you're implying or inferring from this. I knew Alain a long time ago when I was sixteen. We spent three weeks together when we were both in a film. I played the daughter of a respectable family, and he was the Highwayman, whose noble family had fallen on hard times. He kidnapped me down a ladder and carried me off on his horse. He was supposed to hand me over to the villain, Lord Barth — that was an actor called Torren Fairfield — but in the end he couldn't do it. He fought Lord Barth and took me back home."

"And asked for your hand?" Tamzin raised her brows.

"No. I was sixteen, but Marigold, my character, was younger. The Highwayman presented me to my father, swore on his honour that I was *unharmed and unsullied,* told me to be happy, and rode off." She closed her eyes, summoning the long-ago dialogue.

"Shall I ever see you again, Highwayman? And he said, *If the fates wish it, mon souci.* Then he laughed and handed me a posy of marigolds. *Look for me, if you will, at the sign of the marigold . . .* and he blew me a kiss and strode out, ever so swishy, and Hope Gordon, playing Lady Heriot, grabbed my father's arm and shrieked, *After him!* And Hein — Hoffmann, that was, said, *Let him go, my love. Is it not enough that we have our daughter back?* And she said, *He's a criminal! A miscreant! A villain!* And Hein said, *All of those, my lady, but also a man of honour."*

Tamzin broke into a peal of laughter.

"Yes, it was very corny," Pip said cordially, "and maybe that's why it came to be a kind of cult favourite. It was made in the seventies, but more in the style of a golden age melodrama."

"I wasn't laughing at *that.* It was just *you,* becoming all those characters in the space of a few lines."

"Oh, that."

"Oh, that!" Tamzin mimicked. "So what happened next?"

"There's a long shot of Marigold standing in her casement window with the flowers, watching the Highwayman ride away. She raises her flowers to her face — I still remember the smell — then there's a closeup — and she says, *I'll see you again at the sign of the marigold, my Highwayman."*

"So, you must have spent a lot of time with Master Barfleur."

"I did. My old agent, Sully, had warned me of hothouse friendships. They spring up and they're intense, but after you part, they just evaporate."

"It was like that?"

"No. I mean, it wasn't a hothouse friendship. Alain and I were the youngest ones in the cast, but it wasn't even that. We just — liked one another. It was as if we'd been friends forever, and we had so much in common. I don't mean we shared the same experiences — well, obviously not. We laughed at the same things, though. He was so different from the other boys and young men I'd worked with. Not cocky or condescending. He was kind, and he played for me whenever I wanted."

Tamzin said, gently, "You had no idea he was a fairy."

"No. Not consciously. He didn't say and I didn't ask. It never occurred to me to ask."

"I see that."

"Did you know Matin was an elf when you met him?"

"I did, I think. But I knew elves were real. Dequan told me." She might have seen Pip was puzzled, because she added, "Dequan and I were at school together for a couple of years. I'd met elf children and a leprechaun when I was very young. Nanny Lu — Asher's mum — is at least partly an elf, and she was my nanny for a little while. After we moved away from Fiddle Bay, which is more or less where I was born, I never saw Nanny Lu or danced with the elves again until *much* later. I have no memories from that time — not conscious ones — but some good friends helped me to find out what happened and my parents, may their Lycra tarnish, more or less confirmed it once I had them cornered."

"What does this have to do with Dequan?"

"We were at school together, as I said, and the school took us on an excursion to Fiddle Bay. It must have stirred up those old subconscious memories, because I started drawing elves. Dequan and I were talking about it, and he told me there were real elves — I was even at school with some, although we weren't close friends."

"How did he know? He's not one — is he?" She pictured the blond server. He was good-looking, and now she came to think of it, there was a slightly unusual cast to his features.

"He's a trace fay," Tamzin said. "The very traciest of trace fays, he says. His mum is Dutch Australian, and his dad is Chinese Australian — from a family that has lived in Australia since the gold rush days. He looks like his mum."

"Where does the fay come in?"

"His granny — his dad's mum — is the great-granddaughter of a courtfolk man and a Chinese woman — something like that. It's not particularly unusual to have distant fay ancestry. Most people never know, but Granny Juliana used to visit her fay cousins at times, and when Dequan was little she would take him. Anyway, that's how I learned of the fay — but most of my knowledge comes from — "

"The Orders of the Fay," Pip blurted.

Tamzin gave a sudden peal of laughter. "No, Pip. Good guess, but no — most of my knowledge comes from *living over there* for seven years. When I was seventeen, Matin and his friend Otto helped me to escape my parents' web of lies by sending me *over there* to sink or swim. I swam. I had a glorious time, but I never forgot Dequan and I wanted to come back to him. By the time I did, he'd moved on."

"With Tina?"

"No. With a string of lovely women, including one named Annie Blue who is now a good friend of mine as well as a client. I met Matin again by chance and we fell in love, and we were married and had Music — then last year I ran into Dequan at the Patterdale Counterpoint Festival. By then he'd met Tina. They're married now, so everything is wonderful. To get back to Master Barfleur though — what did you think he was?"

"He was my friend. I thought he'd probably been a child performer, like me, and so he'd been home educated or something. He never said. I didn't realise it was his first film. We just—fell into friendship."

"I understand that. If it's not too intrusive, why didn't you keep in touch?"

"I don't remember what happened at the wrap party for *The House of Heriot*. I think I left early with Sully and Little Mum. The others were probably drinking, and it might have got a bit wild. Mobiles weren't a thing, and neither was email. I didn't think to ask exactly where he lived because while we were filming it was a kind of bubble, as if it had no beginning or end. I think I thought it was some posh place—maybe in England even.

"I expected to meet him again sooner or later at a casting call, because everyone said we had good chemistry. When Sully told me he was up for a role in *Pageant Spectacular*, I was pretty excited. I thought it would be the same as before, except I was old enough to—I was in my early twenties. We were both cast in the film, but at separate screen tests, and we never actually met. Missed one another by a day. He left a note for me with the dresser, but when I wrote back via his agent, my letter came back *not known*. And that was that. I never saw or heard from him again until today."

"You didn't ask your agent?"

"No. She'd have just reminded me of *hothouse friendships*."

"So, it must have been a shock to meet him here."

"Not really. We *knew* one another. It's just the same."

"So Matin and I did disturb something."

Pip said, philosophically, "I'm sixty-six and Alain is probably seventyish. I think it's a bit late to *disturb something* where we're concerned. Anyway, how do you know he hasn't got a wife and six fairy sons?"

Tamzin said, "He hasn't. No wife, anyway. Friendship and loving companionship doesn't depend much on age. He's handsome. I was going to say *distinguished looking*, but he

93

looks too user-friendly for that. He still has *it*. Some folk never lose it.

"I met an old seafay man once, at a place called Dawn Island. He was probably in his nineties, and he was mourning his wife. I gave him a kiss in exchange for some drawing paper — a proper one, a *baiser enorm* as a very young friend of mine described it. He didn't take advantage, as he might have done, but I can tell you, he still had *it*. That was the day I started my journey out of fairyland, in as much as I've ever left it. It was also the day I met a new friend."

"The old man?"

"No — his great-granddaughter, Tronda. She gave me a lift in her skiff out to the galleon I was catching to sail home." She paused and added gently, "I knew Tronda for a whole ten minutes, but we're friends. If we lived closer, I'm sure we'd go sailing, and beachcombing, and laugh a lot when we thought of me kissing her great-grandad as a thank-you for a pile of paper. One day I'm going to see her again. Either we'll go off on a galleon and stop at Dawn Island, or else she'll sail that skiff of hers down through the Charm Lines and climb up the path the goats take."

Pip said, "You get it, then. The way it could have been with Alain and me."

"The way it *is* with Alain and you."

"So, how do you know he doesn't have a wife?"

"Easily. See?"

Tamzin held up the series of sketches she'd been making as they conversed.

Pip felt her mouth drop open a little.

Tamzin had apologised, sort of, for sketching her in mid-ballet in the barn when Pip had thought she was alone. This time, she'd caught even more private moments.

There was a brief impression of two people embracing, with the taller one bent over the other.

Tamzin tapped the sketch. "See the way his hands are positioned? That's the way Matin holds me. I assure you it's not the way a married fay man will ever hold another woman. They just—don't."

The other sketches were a series of Pip sitting on the haybale. In the first, her posture was defeated, but she'd unfolded, becoming more animated, happier, hopeful.

Tamzin studied her expression for a while. "I'm sorry," she said.

Pip waved away the apology if that was what it was. "This is not the painting you're doing for your exhibition collection. Please."

"No. Definitely not." Tamzin took back the pad and opened a new page. "It'll have to be a fast one. Shall we have Master Barfleur back so you can chat while I draw?"

"No. Just me. Just the way I am. If you don't mind, I'll be quiet, and list my blessings in alphabetical order."

If Tamzin found that odd, she didn't say so. "Is there any more tea in that pot?"

"Yes. You want some?"

"No, but maybe you do."

Pip took the hint, poured tea, surprisingly still hot, into her festival cup and sipped. She didn't list her blessings after all but sat imagining this was her marigold cup and daydreaming scenes that made her smile.

PART TWO. TASMANIA

May

CHAPTER ONE. VASFED

Pip went home to Lemonwood Cottage.

Settling back into her gently organised life proved both easier and far more difficult than she expected.

The cats were pleased to see her and indulged in much whisker-wiping and crooning. After twenty minutes of such attention, Pip felt almost as slobbered-upon as Lupin's cat.

Is the cocky-leg dog coming to stay? Amberjill wanted to know.

"Which one?" Pip asked.

Clarkia, who had driven her home from the airport, gave her a slight sideways glance and bit her lip.

"Ja? *Und*?" Pip said, raising her eyebrows to her hairline.

"Sorry," Clarkia said.

Pip grinned at her. "No need to be sorry. I was being unnecessarily bolshy. Just take it as read that if I speak and it's not to you, the phone, or some random person in a shop, it's likely to the cats."

Clarkia nodded hastily.

"In fact, let's sort this right now." Pip turned her attention to the cats, two of whom squatted at her feet, taking it in turns to rear up and whisker-whip her knees. "Show Cousin Clarkia that you understand me," she commanded.

Kittisack glanced ferally over his shoulder. *Tell no one.* He then produced his trademark cattish snigger.

Amberjill suggested it might be unwise to let the hoi polloi — where *did* the cats get these weird terms — know of their superior talents.

"Do it," Pip insisted.

The cats signalled that on the whole, they rather thought they wouldn't.

Pip, on the other hand, rather thought they would.

She'd triumphed over a young man in a phone shop who hadn't wanted to sell her a Mark 1 Pink Princess, and against the manager of Jellico Bay Essentials in the matter of stocking Caraway's Comforts. She had prevailed in making Jamie Pendennis reveal his inner dog, *and* in getting him to let her ride home from her Experience in the front seat. She felt the equal of any two cats, fay or not.

"Do it."

They didn't.

On the other hand, Pip thought, she had definitely not prevailed over the kind but clueless stewards who had declined to make proper tea when she flew to Sydney. So maybe . . .

Time to bring out the big guns.

"You two have a choice. Either you can prove to Cousin Clarkia — that's the Cousin Clarkia who feeds you and cossets you and indulges you when I'm not here . . . unless Jamie is here instead — and who lets you sleep on the bed — that I am not a crazed cat lady, or —"

She broke off.

Or what? Kittisack Cat-Morsed with interest.

Pip delivered the *coup de grace*. "*Or* all your meals will henceforth consist of VASFED and water."

Kittisack's whiskers went rigid with shock.

And cheese, Amberjill stated anxiously.

"No cheese. Ever. It's not essential. You will be fed VASFED and water. According to the box, VASFED has got every nutrient a cat needs and probably some that haven't been invented yet."

No cheese?

"No cheese."

The cats looked horrified.

Clarkia asked, "What on earth is VASFED.?"

"*Veterinarian Approved Scientific Feline Entire Diet,*" Pip said. "I believe it's made of lab-created textured vegetable protein with micronutrients and calcium. It is rumoured to be fish-flavoured, but the cats told me, on the one occasion we tried some, that the flavour is more in the nature of sun-warmed vinyl."

Lupin's cat said, gently, *Mistress, there is no need to be cruel to my beloved children.*

"I'm not being cruel," Pip pointed out. "Your beloved children have a choice. They may accede to my reasonable request that will do them no harm and do me some good. In that case they will eat chicken and rice with vegetables and cheese as usual. The other choice is to continue to refuse my reasonable request. If they do that, they will get expensive food guaranteed to make their insides clean enough to eat off and give them flea-defying fur and livers like a day-old kitten's. Either way, they will continue to be fed."

You wouldn't, Amberjill stated. *You would never spend good money on foul food.*

"Oh, but I wouldn't need to. I have an almost full box of the stuff wrapped up in weevil-proof packaging in the pantry."

Kittisack Cat-Morsed urgently, *How shall we provide such proof as you require? I doubt if Mistress Clarkia can read us as you do.*

Pip had been rather afraid of that. She went smoothly to Plan B, speaking directly to Clarkia. "I shall ask them to perform a couple of simple actions. And to avoid any possibility of you thinking I have trained them, I'll let you propose the actions. Just make sure they're physically possible for cats, and things they wouldn't choose to do themselves right at this moment."

Clarkia, staring at the cats in apparent fascination, shook her head. "No need for that."

"Yes there is. Otherwise you'll go on being indulgent while thinking I'm nuts. And I'm not nuts. Not in this respect, anyhow."

Clarkia said, "I didn't mean it that way. I meant, no need to prove it. For heaven's sake, just *look* at them."

Pip looked at them.

"I've never seen cats look so horrified as when you mentioned withholding their cheese. I might have missed seeing that Riley was living a double life for *four years,* but even I'm not blind enough to miss noting that these cats understand you perfectly. And since I have to assume you are more intelligent than cats — then it follows that you understand them just as well."

"Okay," Pip said slowly, "but indulge me. Ask them to do something."

Clarkia shrugged and turned to the cats. "If *you* had been deceived by someone like Riley for four years, what would *you* do? Show me."

The cats rose from their crouched positions and left the kitchen, swaggering their tails. Just before they vanished, they flicked the tips in unison.

Clarkia laughed. "Exactly what I *did* do."

Eventually, she sobered enough to ask, "Would you like me to leave, Pip? I can easily go and stay with Mum and Dad. Not because of your conversational cats, but just because you have chosen to live on your own for years. I expect it was from choice?"

"I never chose. It just happened. Do you want to leave?" Pip asked.

"Not especially. It would feel like a backwards step to go back to the parental home, but I *can.* They'll be nice. I won't be homeless, and anyway, I should be in line for half the sale price of the place down south."

"From my point of view, you're welcome to stay here for

as long as you like," Pip said. "If you don't mind my ballet practice and the cats."

"I *like* the cats, and maybe you could teach me a bit of dancing. It's good exercise, right?" Clarkia said.

The goat ballet, *Caprice,* which had never left the recesses of Pip's mind since she had mentioned it briefly to Costas, flexed its hooves at her. If she could teach basic steps to her novice cousin, maybe they *could* have a word with the school. After *Queen of the Clowder*, she had developed a thirst for more dancing with purpose. The Almaclairs wanted her to go to demonstrate *Queen* at some point, but they hadn't yet set a date.

She said, "I'm planning to unpack some boxes and crates. They've been in the west room since I moved in, and if we sort them out, and toss or donate what isn't needed, we could get you a good bed, and you could do the room up any way you like. I might need to go away again in July, if not sooner." She remembered abruptly that Clarkia might also be involved in the book launch during Tales in Tune—if it happened—and hastened to add, "but if you can't stay with the cats at any time when I'm not here, it will be fine. I have a friend whose nephew is happy to cat-sit. He's done it before and the cats like him, and his dog."

Clarkia relaxed. "Staying on for a bit would be wonderful if you mean it. I love the town here, and I've been offered a bit of work at Jelly-and-Juice. Wanda's pregnant, and not well at all. I could help you with the boxes . . . as soon as you want."

Pip felt relieved. She'd always known she should unpack those crates, but as the years passed it had become easier to leave them as they were. Now she had a good reason to clear some of her past. She could choose to display it, sell it, donate it, or . . . re-box it. With Clarkia's input it would be easier. After all, Clarkia was her natural heir, in as much as she had one.

Besides, she had told Alain she would do it soon. Soon was now.

She got up abruptly. "Let's unpack the first one. I want to find some catalogues that used to belong to Little Mum, so we'll start by looking for those."

Clarkia said, "Er—don't you need a rest, Pip? You've only just got home, and I expect you've been pretty busy with the film."

Pip thought of the packed days at the festival, of dancing the whole hour, twice daily, filming almost every scene of *Half-Life of the Lost*, rehearsing one ballet and trying to keep abreast of another, of making friends with Star and Candlemas and Laura, keeping up with Jane, rediscovering Tamzin and meeting Alain again. She almost laughed at the thought of being tired after sitting in a plane for a couple of hours and in a car for a couple more, but instead she just said sedately that she was fine, thank you . . . and headed for the west room to open boxes.

Maybe she'd flop tomorrow but today she'd run on whatever adrenalin was left in the tank.

Chapter Two. Last Cat Standing

The boxes and crates occupied Pip and Clarkia for some time. They occupied the cats, too. Kittisack and Amberjill spent hours pouncing and delving, clawing shavings and decade-old newspapers and kneading them into temporary beds.

Rather than take a scattergun approach, they started with the closest crate and methodically emptied that, sorted the contents into heaps, then dealt with the heaps accordingly. Pip acquired four large baskets for the piles, and labelled them — toss, re-box, donate, display. As soon as each was full, they would stop work and dispense with the contents appropriately.

On the third day, Clarkia pried open a crate with a pinch bar she'd acquired from someone called Dave at the service station on the same day Pip got the baskets from Essentials.

Pip frowned, disremembering anyone of that name. The surly mechanic was called Smitt, she thought. Not that he was born surly, she supposed, but he surely was when confronted by her little runabout. He wanted to replace the shockies because one of them squeaked. He also wanted to do a respray because one wing was faded, and the left hind quarter had come from a different car. Pip did not want him to do either of these things. They'd had *words*.

The pinch bar was pink.

Pip indicated it as the nails shrieked free of the wood they'd clasped for eleven years and counting. "Ja. *Und?*"

Clarkia laughed. "Just Dave's little joke. She likes to scandalise her uncle."

So Dave was a girl. Davina, possibly. Someone else was

called Davina, too. Pip wrinkled her brow and wrestled with her memory, jam-packed with images of her glorious festival week.

Ah! Edgar and Joan Treadwell had a relative with that name, who had produced a baby. That was it.

She glanced affectionately at the Treadwell bucket, lately the repository of her marigolds from Gillan but now embracing raffia and nails. She loved the Treadwell bucket.

She'd loved the marigolds, too, but quarantine regulations forbade her from flying them back to Tasmania, and anyway, they had begun to fade. She'd given them to Tamzin, who had said she'd try to strike some cuttings for her painter's garden.

Pip liked the idea of some of her marigolds growing on Delphinium Island. As with the Heaven and Earth ring which she had left at the fossmere, she was drawn to the notion of connecting things and places she loved.

I'll plant some legal seedlings here, she decided. All sorts. French and African and pot marigold. I'll have a bed of tawny orange and lemon gold right next to the camomile, then some of those brown and red chrysanthemums, and some nasturtiums.

She couldn't wait—but she'd have to. The autumn was progressing, and it was too late to plant frost-sensitive things such as nasturtiums. She supposed she could start some marigold seeds in pots, though.

Clarkia finished removing the nails from the wood and laid aside the lid.

Inside the crate was a layer of newspaper, and under that was an explosion of colour.

"Wow!" Clarkia said.

Pip took out some of the catalogues, pleased to have found them. "Most of these are probably from *Marieke's Kleine Nederlanden*, over at West Cape. There will be some from *Pansy That* and maybe from *Bloomin' Likely*. Little Mum loved her catalogues." She shuffled the thick pages of possibility. There should be one . . . Ah!"

Her hands shook a wee bit as she cut one out from the bunch. Clarkia took possession of the others, and was soon leafing through them, apparently absorbed.

Pip paged to the middle of Autumn 2012, opening out the checkerboard green of the order form.

There it was, in Little Mum's loopy script, neatly written out. *Three dozen random mixed Firebird Tulips.* The order form had been torn out and enclosed back in the catalogue along with an addressed envelope.

Out of sight, out of mind.

Pip's mind fled back to that last day with Little Mum.

"Pip, would you get this into the post for me today?"

"Okay. Can I get you anything else?"

"No, love. But do make sure you catch the mail. I should have ordered these last week. They really need to be in the ground by May Day. I've been slack."

"I'll take it after lunch."

"Thanks, love. And you might get a wee can of TunaYum for Duster. He doesn't seem to fancy his dinner lately. Might warrant a vet trip, but I think it's just old age."

Duster, or Last Cat Standing as Pip sometimes thought of him, had been seventeen, a venerable age for a venerable cat. He was a grave and dignified presence, always with Little Mum. He was sole survivor of the ramshackle parade of dogs, cats, and guineapigs that had shared the old family home with the Pearmains since before Pip was born. Six months before, when the second-last cat standing died, Little Mum had been offered a kitten by a sympathetic neighbour. Unusually, she'd refused.

"I think Duster is too old to be pestered with paws and patterings now. Maybe later."

Pip had been going to suggest Duster would be even older then when she'd realised what Little Mum meant.

Little Mum loved Duster, as she had loved every one of the ramshackle parade, but she was never sentimental.

Neither was Pip.

And yet, seeing Little Mum's writing, and remembering her looking forward to bright frilled and fringed Firebird tulips in the spring, and possibly to a kitten then as well brought a hot gush of tears.

Despite her promise to Little Mum, she'd never posted that order.

She would post it now.

To be sure, the catalogue was ten years old, and maybe the tulip farm at West Cape no longer stocked Firebird tulips. They certainly wouldn't be available for the same price.

Pip put the order form in the envelope and inspected it. The 45-cent stamp was outmoded. The cost of local postage had more than doubled. Pip found three 20s and a 5 and stuck them on to make up the balance. She enclosed a note written in her miniscule script, explaining that she knew the price would have changed, and asking for email confirmation of the correct amount to be added.

Then she left Clarkia to her perusal of tulips of every available colour and slipped off to the post office.

There you go, Little Mum . . . it caught the afternoon post just as I promised.

Now it was in the lap of whatever godlets looked after tardy daughters.

Pip twisted the ring of kindness on her finger, hoping fervently for the best. Then she returned to make herself tea, which she drank from her marigold cup.

She smiled, thinking of Alain, maybe standing in the middle of a stately kitchen, also drinking tea and thinking of his old friend Pippin.

If I could snap my fingers and be with him . . .

She rinsed the cup along with Clarkia's and returned to the interminable crates.

Chapter Three. The Acid Test

A n answer came much sooner than Pip had hoped. West Cape was just a few hours away by car, but mail times were unpredictable.

It came as a friendly email, saying that indeed they remembered Rosie Pearmain who had been an honoured and frequent customer, that they would forward the tulips immediately, and asking if they should go to the usual address.

Oops. Pip had added extra stamps, but she must have neglected to change the old Delmsford address on the back of the envelope. Whatever would the new owner think if a parcel of bulbs arrived out of the blue?

She emailed back, apologising and asking for them to be sent to her new Jellico Bay address.

By return of mail, the tulip farm responded with a plump, padded bag of prospective life. *Get them in as soon as you can. If you're too late, they might not bloom this year.*

Pip, assured of the bulbs' reality, keyed in Star Calder-Quince's number, choosing a time when Clarkia had gone to take a shift at Jelly-and-Juice.

"Hello?"

"Star?" Pip responded.

"No."

"Um—Candlemas?"

"No."

"Who are you then?" Pip asked.

"Pentecost," the voice responded.

Pentecost? But then, why not?

"I want to speak to Star," Pip pressed on.

A muffled altercation followed before Star, sounding exasperated, came on the line. "Hello? Go *away*, Pente, and take Trinny with you. Now! Sorry—um—what can I do for you? Kids—I ask you!"

"Ja. *Und?*"

After a short and startled silence, Star laughed. "Pippin Pearmain—how are you?"

"Okay," Pip said. She rocked on her toes. She and Star had been good friends during *Dance in Tune,* but she was unsure if the friendship would survive their return to their very different lives.

Hothouse friendships were real. She didn't think she and Star had one, but this was the acid test.

She realised Star was waiting to know why she'd called, and suspected she was getting impatient. This was possibly a bad idea.

She was going to apologise and hang up when Star said, "All set for our trip to Patterdale?"

Pip dredged in her memory. Ah! That was where the Forever dance troupe had its headquarters. "I haven't had any confirmation of that yet."

"Neither have I, officially, but Candlemas heard from Jane, who had it from Laura, who said Richenda told her it was going ahead. The girly-vine I call it. Candle's forever on the phone with one or the other of them—though not Jane, actually, for some reason. I have a feeling she lives off the grid—"

You don't know the half of it.

"Anyway, if it wasn't that—"

Pip blurted, "I ordered the Firebirds and they've arrived."

"The—"

"The Firebird tulips. For—"

"For your mum!" Star sounded as if she was grinning. "When do you want to do this? I'll book the flight right away. Have to be a flying visit, though—the Bibs are in rehearsal for

The Sandbox. I'm playing Squid."

"Never mind, then. Obviously —"

"Pip, I'm coming. This clandestine planting absolutely needs to happen, and I want to be part of it. I'm looking up Delmsford as we speak, and I see there's a sunset flight that lands me a couple of hours away. I can hire a car, or —"

"I'll pick you up from the airport," Pip said firmly.

"Are you sure? It's not near where you live now, is it."

"No, but the airport is a triangulation between here and Delmsford. Practically on the way. If you get in at seven, I can get us to the old house by nine and we can have supper at the pub. They always used to do marvellous suppers. Then —"

"Then we do the deed by moonlight and pull an all-nighter. Or, more sensibly, you can drop me back at the airport and I'll settle in and catch the milk-run home. There's a flight going out at five. Cheap as! And . . . I've . . . booked it! Easy-peasy."

It sounded anything but easy-peasy to Pip, but Star seemed positively jovial at the idea of flying in and out of the state in the space of a few hours.

"What day?" she asked hurriedly.

"Full moon — May sixteen. It's a bit late, but the point is to get them in. Can you bring the tools?"

"Yes," Pip answered.

"Grand. See you then." Star hung up.

Kittisack wound his tail around Pip's ankle, making her jump.

What are you doing under the full moon?

"Planting tulips," Pip said. "At night, at the house where I used to live, with someone I met last month who is flying in for the night."

A goodly endeavour, the original cat approved. *We applaud the notion, and we shall be in attendance.*

Pip didn't believe that, but Lupin's cat signalled gently that it would be so, and that there was no need for her to be troubled.

Pip had the impression the guardian was laughing at her.

CHAPTER FOUR. FAMILY IS WHAT MATTERS IN THE END

At the airport, Pip wondered if she'd recognise Star. Not that she was afflicted with Humph's odd condition that made him so poor at facial recognition, but more because she'd known Star for such a short and specific time. She'd seen her only in costume or in festival clothing. The same applied to Star's recognition of Pip, but at least she was small enough to be memorable.

She parked in the overflow and waited anxiously as passengers came up from the apron.

There weren't many. It was an unpopular time to fly.

There she is.

Star carried a small backpack with a pair of floral gardening gloves and a giant torch attached.

To Pip, it positively shouted "moonlit escapade."

Star's eyes crinkled in welcome as she spotted Pip.

"Aha, my partner in crime, dressed for dauntless derring-do. I was afraid you might have chickened out."

"I said I'd be here."

"I know. I must be *me of little faith*. Of course you're here. Have you heard from the Forevers yet?"

Pip nodded. "Mid-June, so Magda said. She's not coming. She said she thinks I'm old enough to look after myself. She's promised to let me know of any opportunity that comes up, though — in the performance line. I'm sure she will. She's actively putting me up for roles."

"My word, aren't we a jet-setting couple! Candlemas is nearly turning herself inside out and Trinny and Pente are as cross as can be that they didn't volunteer at the festival. Humph is coming with us, by the way. He's keen to reprise Dappercat and he's bought a new top hat with custom ears and new shoes from an odd little business called The Cobbler. It's run by a woman called Máiréad something or other. I think she's Irish. Maybe we could all meet up at the airport."

"Maybe," Pip said. Her brain felt as if it was trying to expand from what she considered *Lemonwood normal* to the faster-paced and utterly crammed state of Dance in Tune.

She ushered Star out of the lit-up airport and into the halogen lighting of the overflow. "That's my car," she said, indicating it. She opened the passenger door, which stuck as usual, for Star and got herself in. "We can stop off on the way if you need to."

"I'll be fine." Star looked up at the twinkling sky, where a full moon hung. "This is fun. I'm so glad we got to do it."

Pip didn't reply. She wasn't sure how she felt as old, current and new lives clashed and merged.

Immerse yourself in the experience, Kittisack intoned from his perch in the back seat.

Hush, you.

Despite Clarkia's suspension of disbelief. Pip found it easier to converse with the cats in silence most of the time. It worked well.

As Pip pulled out onto the highway, Star turned to put her bag in the seat behind.

"Crikey! You brought the cats!"

"Yes," Pip said, as nonchalantly as she could.

Star gave a little sitting-down jiggle. "Pip, my dear, you're utterly mad. That's probably why I like you so much. I've always wanted someone to be mad with. Rox is not it, bless him—far too responsible. Pente and Trinny are at the scornful and superior stage. They address me as Mo-*ther* with sighs to make Dame Billie Clarty weep with envy. Did you ever work with Dame Billie?"

"No."

"Neither did I, but she's a *legend*. I catch her plays whenever it's practical. Mind, I have hopes of Candlemas."

So did Pip. She said, without premeditation, "She's a nudger."

"Oho, so you noticed that, did you?" Star chuckled. "She looks so wide-eyed and innocent, and yet she can get people to do things in a way you would never expect."

"Jane's like that."

"I saw. Fortunately, Candlemas is innately kind, so she shouldn't get *too* manipulative. I wouldn't be surprised if she's a principal ballerina — though she ought to have started earlier for that — or a captain of industry, or the president of a charity — oh dear. She'd love this little enterprise of ours, but I'm being selfish. You and I deserve it and if I'd brought Candle, I'd have had to trouble myself about the possibility of blighting her future if we get caught."

Amberjill Cat-Morsed, *We'll be with you.*

Pip wondered what that was meant to imply.

Driving into Delmsford, even at night, brought a flood of nostalgia. Crossing the hollow-sounding bridge over the River Delm gave Pip a prickle of awareness.

"I used to climb down the pylons and swim under the bridge when I was young," she told Star.

"Did your mum mind?"

"Mum didn't know. I did it with Lupin and Juniper. We had a *tell no one* pact, mainly to protect Lupin."

"A sensitive soul?"

"Lord, no! Lupin was the original sergeant major! She was four years older than me, and I'm two years older than Jan — that's Juniper — and so we younger ones were allowed a ridiculous amount of freedom, as long as we were with Lupin. It made sense for us to uphold the image of protective custody. If our parents had known what we really got up to . . ." She shrugged. "Lupin made the rules. *If I wouldn't do it, we don't do it.* Fortunately, there wasn't much Lupin wouldn't do. I was never brave, but I always felt safe with Loopy Lou calling the shots."

"You must miss her," Star said.

"How did—"

"You refer to her in the past tense."

"I do miss her, I suppose. I'd seen her just once since two-thousand and twelve, but she was always *there.* On the back roads of my mind. Do you have cousins?"

"Only the one firstie on Mum's side, and some more distant ones on Dad's," Star said. "Ooh, a pub! Can we?"

Pip glanced at the dashboard clock. "Yes, let's. I'd take you for a town tour, but it's dark."

"I'll come back in summer, and we'll have a good prowl," Star said cheerfully. "Maybe your cousin might come and you two can go down Memory Road and take me along for the ride."

"I'll ask her." Pip pulled into the carpark of the Waybridge Hotel and switched off the engine.

"Is she like you?"

"Not a bit. But we're family."

"Family is what matters in the end," Star said. "I remember when Rox became *family.* So many couples break up because *the magic's gone* or some such idiocy. *I* think they're missing the point. When you're in love, in the early days, you don't notice the feet of clay or the dirty socks. Then, when you're a couple and neither of you bothers to look anywhere else, the quirks start to annoy you. After that, if you stick it out, they become just a part of the other person, then you find you've transitioned into *family.* It's nice."

Pip remembered. Little Mum and Little Dad had been like that.

She got out of the car. "You two, behave," she said to the cats.

Bring us cheese, they Cat-Morsed in militant chorus.

Chapter Five. Pizza

The Waybridge had changed its décor and updated its menu in the years since Pip had been there for Saturday supper.

Pip ordered salmon with a seasonal vegetable medley. When it arrived, she looked doubtfully at the crossed carrot spears propped against a single floret of cauliflower. Three green beans had been formed into a kind of triskelion on top of a piece of salmon the size of a matchbox. There were two curls of red pepper and a third curl of something that might be candied ginger.

"Enjoy your meal," the server murmured, after giving three grinds of pepper to each plate. She had elbow-length black sleeves, black leggings, and an apron. She looked as depressed as the meal.

Pip wanted to raise Cain, but her shamed memory of the fuss she'd made regarding tea-making on the plane to Sydney persuaded her to hold her tongue.

"It tastes okay," Star allowed, putting down her cutlery. "Good, actually." She grinned at Pip. "Is there a fish-and-chippy here?"

"There used to be, but they always closed at seven."

"Dammit. A pizza place?"

"The pub does pizza," a fellow diner called to them.

"Is their Family Pizza bigger than a playing card?" Star asked, giving him the benefit of her big smile.

"Dinner plate sized. Plenty of topping. I commend you to the chicken, cheese, and wilted spinach."

"Grand, we'll have one."

Star caught the server's eye. "Can you bring us a pizza, please? What he said." She gestured to the diner.

The server gave her a pained assent.

The diner chuckled, tossing back his corkscrew black curls. They were so messy Pip couldn't decide whether they were natural or whether he'd spent the price of a year's electrics bill at the hairdresser. His eyes were borage blue. She suspected he wore contacts. She'd never seen anyone with eyes that colour before.

"Told you, Georgia," he said to the server. "You can't get away with micro-dine in Delmsford. It just won't fly."

"That's a bit unkind," Star responded after the server had vanished. "It was delightful salmon — but we've come a long way and we're hungry."

"Pub meals ought to know their place," the diner said. He got up and approached their table. "Are you ladies doing anything later? We could reconvene at the bar and set the world to rights, one dish at a time."

"We're booked out," Star said. "I'll be talking to my husband and my friend will be taking two cats for a drive."

"Point taken. You don't associate with strangers." He looked from one to the other. "I'm Rafferty Kettle for *Fodder International*. Write that down, or stick it in your phones, so next time we meet we won't *be* strangers and we can go to the bar. Husbands and cats included, naturally. I don't hold with trespassing. You are?"

"I'm Star. She's Pippin."

"Perfect. I made a bet with myself that you weren't called Susan and Michelle. Enjoy your supplementary pizza, Star and Pippin. I did!"

He left the pub, curls bouncing with energy. Star gazed after him. "Cheeky git. And *not* a local, I'm thinking."

"He is, actually, as of recently," the server said returning with a pizza on a wooden board.

"That was quick," Star said, sounding impressed.

"Got a pile of them prepped to go." The server sounded resigned. "Dad's ready to throw in the towel—if not the whole load of laundry. See, these days, you've got to have an angle. If you can run to a historical bushranger, or gold panning, or tree houses, or bush tucker, it's all good, but *Delmsford*? I ask you, what the devil is unique to Delmsford? You can't even do anything with the name. It's built on the River Delm, but the original River Delm is in Essex, and everyone mixes it up with Chelmsford. There's not even a ford here. It's a transplanted name."

"So you decided to go minimalist," Star said, cutting across what sounded to Pip like an often-rehearsed grumble.

"Got to do something. It doesn't even save money. All that fine dining costs an arm and a leg."

"You could be the pizza pub," Pip said. "This looks really good."

"Or full-on retro with fish and chips, pizza, chicken parmi, roast and veg, sausage and mash and soup and damper on rotation," Star suggested.

"You might be in on an idea there, but Dad likes his culture."

"We could set a ballet here," Pip said thoughtfully. "Or a musical play—"

"A—" The server looked hard at Pip. "Um . . . do I know you from somewhere?"

"Probably from the telly," Star said. "She's been in lots of series."

"But not lately," Pip said.

"Not telly—dancing. Did you ever come to the Delmsford Hall and dance with playgroup kids?"

"You remember that?"

The server laughed. "Not much. I was only three or four.

I've got a picture though — I'm wearing a party frock my god-mother sent over from England, just like in that old children's book where English kids put on a pageant. Dancing days were the only times I got to wear it, so Mum cut the picture out of the paper and had it framed. You're in it, and so's a kid with wavy hair — Andie Lake, I think it says. I don't remember her, but I sort of remember you. Apparently you used to come nearly every week, but then you just — stopped."

"Pip's a performer, so maybe she got a part," Star said. "As it happened we've both just finished filming a movie. *And* we premiered a ballet."

"So, you two are famous and you're sitting here eating pizza in *our* pub." The server shook her head. "I guess we could go for *Pub to the Stars* as our theme. Have to run it past Dad. Maybe you could recommend us to some other telly people? We could name the pizzas after famous people who ordered them."

Pip remembered something. "Can I have a couple of slices of cheese to go?"

"Not enough on the pizza?"

"Plenty on the pizza. This is for my cats."

"Cats can't digest cheese."

"These cats can," Pip said.

The server brought a selection of cheese in a small cardboard box. "What are your names? Would I have heard of you?"

"Doubt it. I'm Pippin Pearmain and she's Star Calder-Quince."

"Pearmain — did you used to live with the nice old lady at Treasures?"

Pip assented. "But I moved ages ago."

They left the pub.

Star puffed out her cheeks. "Nothing like a country pub for showing how ordinary you really are. I'm guessing the old lady was your mum?"

"Yes, I expect so."

"It killed an hour, anyway. Is there anywhere else we can go until it's time to plant our plunder?"

Pip gave cheese to the cats, who responded with purrs of pleasure. *Mozzarella,* Kittisack announced, but Amberjill opined it was a local red Leicester.

Again, Pip wondered how on earth they knew. She glanced at the dashboard clock.

"It's nearly ten o'clock. I should think we could go now. The moon's up."

"Right. It might seem less fishy if we're wandering around at ten rather than after midnight. Do we drive there?"

"We can easily walk. It's not far, and it'll give our eyes a chance to adjust."

Chapter Six. Firebirds

Pip opened the boot of her runabout. She lifted out the Treadwell bucket and handed it to Star. "Firebird tulips— three dozen." She took out a couple of trowels and a bag of compost, and a short-handled hoe, and garden fork. "These used to be Little Mum's. She had them made especially because the commercial ones were all too big and the ones made for children were too puny."

Star took possession of the hoe and a trowel, and they set off.

Just like *The Twins with the Bucket of Bulbs*, Pip mused, remembering a story from Grandmother's Sunshine. She and Star were not children, or twins, but they certainly had a bucket of bulbs.

"We ought to be carrying this bucket Jack-and-Jill fashion," she remarked.

"Snap! Just what I was thinking," Star said. "Want to try?"

"Too much height difference," Pip decided. "Anyhow, it isn't heavy."

They had walked for three or four minutes when Pip became aware the cats were with them, flitting along like ghosts.

She was fairly sure she'd left the windows up in the car. It was late autumn, and certainly not hot enough for the cats to be uncomfortable in the vehicle at night.

Kittisack?

Tell no one. And call me the original cat.

Pip said, without sound, *Are you trying to freak Star out?*

Amberjill purred, *We like Star. She is an excellent choice for*

121

this endeavour.

Pip agreed, but she had no clue why the cats thought so, or why they were interested at all, for that matter. It was not as if they'd ever known Little Mum.

Cattish laughter dinned in her mental ears. *Of course we knew her.*

Pip's shoulder blades prickled with unease. Occasionally, the cats were just too creepy for words.

She said nothing aloud, hoping Star might not notice their covert escort.

They reached the turnoff to the lane leading into Treasures, the house where Pip had lived for fifty-five years. It wasn't the original family homestead — that had been where Little Nanna and Little Pop Laurel lived, up on the hill — and it was less imposing than the name suggested.

"It's just a three-bedroom fifties brick house," Pip explained as they turned into the familiar lane. "Little Dad built it with one of those war-service loans. But it's on a triple block, because the third one is an odd shape, so Dad got it cheap."

"That explains the big garden, then," Star said.

"Yes. There were chooks and ducks, and a small pond in the extra block."

"That might be the place to put the tulips," Star opined.

"It was never a flower garden. Little Mum used to have the spring bulbs near the house. I want to put them among other bulbs."

"Any particular reason?" Star dropped her voice.

"Yes." Pip dropped hers as well. "I never thought of this while we were planning, but tulips are toxic to cats and dogs. I know Kittisack and Amberjill wouldn't eat them, but some others might. If I put them with an existing planting I won't be causing any danger that didn't exist already."

"I never thought of that either. It's one thing to have an escapade, but I wouldn't ever want to do harm. What *were* we thinking?"

"It will be okay if we add to an existing planting."

"But how will you *know* there's an existing planting?" Star asked, sounding amused. "It's dark."

"I'll take a chance that the owners have left the garden design more or less the same. It takes a hard heart to dig up a bed of daffodils, paperwhites, freesias, hyacinths, and snowflakes—and if you don't like flowers, why buy a big garden with old and extensive plantings? There's a huge rose bed too . . . or there was. The garden runs right along the main road, but this lane takes us to the back of the house."

"Do you know the people who live here?"

"No. Not even their names. I sold it through an agent. I didn't want to know," Pip confessed. She winced as she remembered her flit to Jellico Bay when it all became Too Much.

She opened the small wooden gate, still painted white, according to the moonlight. Her fingers found the latch as if she still lived there.

The house was dark. A van of some kind was parked in the open double garage.

Pip led the way around to the side of the house. "Does your torch have a dimmer?" she asked softly.

"I don't think so."

"Okay." Pip bent to look closely at the mulched ground.

Amberjill flitted past her, light as a leaf, and pawed at the rustling mulch.

Hyacinths, she reported.

Kittisack wiped his whiskers down a precocious shoot. *Scylla.*

Pip relaxed as the cats skulked off under the trees. Little Mum hadn't grown scylla, preferring English bluebells and Scottish harebells, so the bed must have been augmented rather than reduced or replaced.

She put down her tools and felt for the edging of river rocks Little Mum had used for a mowing strip.

Still there. Good. Whoever lives here now is a status quo person.

"If we shift these outwards a bit we can plant the tulips as a new border without disturbing anything else."

She lifted a stone to the right as demonstration.

Star knelt to help her.

When they had the edging moved, Pip plied her trowel. Star worked from the other end with the hoe and broke up the clods with the fork. Soon they had a small trench. Pip scattered in the well-rotted compost and lime she had brought.

Star picked up the bucket of bulbs and brought it to the middle of the trench. "I feel as if I'm in a fairy tale." She put down the bucket and stretched her back. "I thought I was fit, but all that stooping is making me creak. However do you do that hoop bend?"

"At my age, you mean?"

"At any age!"

Pip shrugged. "You have farther to bend than I do."

"We have the same number of vertebrae, so that shouldn't matter."

"Yours are farther apart. Anyway, I've seen you do calf stretches and hoop bends."

"Yes, but I can't stay down there for ten minutes. Thirty seconds is my lot. Now what are you up to?" Star asked as Pip started rummaging under the tree.

"Collecting leaves. If we scatter them over the edging stones, with luck no one will notice they've been moved. We don't want them rolling the rocks back into position and squishing the bulbs."

"Crikey no!" Star came to help her pile leaves into the Treadwell bucket.

They had almost finished their camouflage work when they heard the click of the latch and someone on the path. They froze under the trees.

CHAPTER SEVEN. SISTERS IN CRIME

W hoever was on the path whistled a tune, doing it well, with trills and warbles.

Pip held her breath. She was aware of Star gasping with silent giggles beside her.

The whistler walked up the steps. A security light came on, illuminating him as he pushed his key into the lock.

Star gave an almost silent intake of breath. "It's the unbelievable pizza guy."

Pip bit her lip. It was indeed the pizza guy, Rafferty Kettle. He'd seemed friendly, but whatever would he think if he found the women from the pub spanneling around in his garden? If it was his garden . . . Maybe he was visiting and had been given a key.

Pip didn't much care what people thought of her, but still . . .

Star moved and put her foot on a concealed edging stone. She sidestepped, bumping into Pip.

Pizza Guy paused with the key still in the lock. "Who's there?"

A weird wail from overhead made Pip cringe.

Another followed, then two small bodies hit the ground and fled into the next garden, hissing and spitting.

"Blasted cats." Pizza Guy sounded quite good humoured. He let himself in and closed the door.

Star let out her breath in a shaky sigh. "Thought we were goners," she said,

So had Pip. They waited a few minutes. The security light

went off. Evidently one had to be on the steps for it to come on. A light illuminated one of the rooms, dimmed by red curtains. They were new, anyway. Little Mum's had been cream linen with ghostly florals.

When their eyes recovered from the light, they scattered the rest of the leaves from the bucket and retrieved their belongings, making a meticulous accounting of tools before creeping out into the lane.

They headed back towards the Waybridge Hotel which was now in darkness.

"We ought to have left a calling card," Star said. "Star and Pippin were here!"

"We might have if you hadn't introduced us by name."

"Pearmain and Calder-Quince were here!"

"A bit memorable. I know there are very few Pearmains — and none at all that I know of related to me — and Calder-Quince can't be common either."

"I think we're the only ones . . . Rox's family, I mean. His grandfather Calder married a powerful lady — think Humph's Gwen on steroids — She refused to *Calder* herself and Grandpa wouldn't make a *Quince* of himself. They might have called the whole thing off, but instead they chose to hyphenate. Evidently they drew straws to see which name went first.

"Rox, bless him, offered to join me as a Fortunato, but I decided to take my chances with Calder-Quince. Roxburghe Fortunato sounds like Victorian cad, and besides, I was a bit fed up with being thrown out of casting calls because I didn't *look* Italian. Of course I didn't. I'm not!"

Pip shook her head, mildly confused.

"Dad *assumed* it," Star said cheerfully. "Fortunato, I mean. He's a magician. The Great Fortunato!" She laughed. "That's one reason I can lie so still. I was his assistant when I was in my teens, and one of my party-pieces was as Medusa's

Victim—frozen in horror." Star assumed a startled dagger-fingered pose before relaxing to herself again. "Dad deed-polled himself before he married Mum, so *Fortunato was I born* rather than being tied to his original name."

"What was that?"

"Parr. Truly. Can you imagine me going through life with a name like Star Parr? Neither can I. I tell you, dear Pippin— *you couldn't make it up!*"

"In that case we definitely can't go back and leave a *We wuz here* sign," Pip said. "Anyway, *we* know we were there."

Star murmured assent as she contemplated Pip's runabout and brushed at her knees. "I'm thinking you won't mind a bit of leaf mould in your car."

"Not a bit," Pip said.

"And I'm further thinking a small celebration is in order." Star scrabbled in her backpack and removed a small bottle and a leather case that might once have contained binoculars. She opened that and took out two little stemless glasses the size of eggcups. "These belonged to an ancestor," she said. "And *this*, believe it or not, is a wee dram of the original recipe *Caraway's Cordial*. It's special order—and not one of the commercial lines. It's non-alcoholic, but that's as much as I can tell you, so if you have any weird food allergies inform me now."

"I don't," Pip said.

Star removed the cork from the bottle and poured a little liquid into each glass. "Some people water it down, but *we* drink it neat as the original Caraway probably intended. Bottoms up! To your Little Mum and her Firebird tulips, and to never growing too old to want to dance the full hour!"

"To Little Mum!" Pip said.

Star passed her a glass, and they drank together.

To Pip, a veteran of eyewatering juice from the sentient lemon and Nanna Laurel's more tongue-withering concoctions, the Caraway's Cordial tasted surprisingly pleasant. She thought it had clover in it, probably honey, and one of the more robust extracts — liquorice or anise. Prune juice . . . maybe. Elderflower — certainly. With those ingredients, it would have some kind of gentle tonic effect, as was originally intended.

"I like that." She handed the glass back to Star, who dried it efficiently with the tail of her shirt and put it away.

"Wash them later," she said. "Phew! I was worried about getting that through the quarantine. Ridiculous, since it's utterly harmless."

"Rather good for you, I expect," Pip said. "You said you don't sell it?"

"We-11, not to say *sell* it, but the company does have limited editions for Gold subscribers."

"You mean I could have been a subscriber all these years? A *Gold* subscriber?" Pip was already a Super Pager with *The Orange Grove*. Now she had another ambition to lust for.

Star said, "Yes, if you bought directly from our catalogue and gained enough points. Where do you get your supplies at present?"

"Little Mum used to buy from the Lavender Ladies' Emporium. Later, I got things online from *Lather and Bubbles*. I — er — persuaded the Essentials shop where I live to start stocking it, but they do have a limited range. It's difficult in the smaller country towns. Unit cost is a problem and buying in bulk means storage issues."

Star looked at her in amusement. "You're not wrong there. At some point in the seventies Caraway's trialled a sort of party plan for country areas."

"Were you even born then?"

"Yes. Just. It was wildly successful for a few months, but the stuff goes so far people needed to buy it only every three months or so, and it was difficult to consistently find new clients in the country. The next idea was the catalogue and that still works today. I'm surprised you didn't know. I'll put one in the post for you tomorrow — or send you to Caraway's online."

"Please do." Pip felt invigorated. They'd completed their planned escapade *and* she could get her Caraway's Comforts without battling Mister Essentials. She would have access to limited editions. She could become a *gold subscriber*. Maybe there was a badge. She frowned. *The Orange Grove* didn't offer badges for its Super Pagers. It should. Despite the long line of plush cats and diamante bracelets, the last badges Pip remembered were when she'd belonged to the Possum Club. Nanna Laurel had been Boss Poss, and that meant Pip had to be *extra* good at things to earn her badges.

Must suggest an orange badge . . . or maybe one with trees, and with branches you can add.

"I'll come back here in spring to see if they're flowering," she said, leaving oranges behind and reverting briefly to the firebirds.

"If they are, will you send me a photo?" Star asked, also shifting seamlessly. She was good at that.

"Of course." Pip opened the passenger door.

"Weren't we going to do a dance of dedication?" Star asked.

"Something like that, but the pizza guy put it out of my mind. Never mind. We drank to their health, and I'll dance for them when they're in flower."

You took your time. The Cat-Morse from Kittisack was indulgent.

We had insufficient cheese, Amberjill added.

Pip said, "Then it's just as well I brought you some extra slices. I believe you'll find a mild Colby and some local Delmsford minted Cheddar in the selection."

Star said, "Um?"

Pip gave the cats more cheese and said, "Where to now? You could come back to my place to get some sleep, but it would have to be the couch. My cousin Clarkia is in the west room, half concealed by boxes."

Star yawned. "It must be getting on for midnight, so it wouldn't be worth it. Just take me back to the airport, and I'll kip on one of the couches. I can sleep anywhere. I'm famous for it."

"Okay." Pip wasn't sure if she was disappointed or relieved. "I'll take you back, but I'll hang round in case you're not allowed to sleep there or something. It's not Melbourne. I'm not sure if there's even an airport hotel."

"I'll be fine." Star sounded amused. "I can always do callisthenics all night and sleep on the plane."

Nevertheless, Pip elected to drive around for a while, spending more petrol than she'd probably used in the past six months.

As the time before Star's flight shrank from four hours to three, Pip realised they'd been talking almost non-stop.

She finally drove back to the airport, parked and walked in.

The place was lit up. It was almost empty apart from a couple of staff sitting sleepily in the café.

"I'll go and get some coffee," Star said. She looked down at Pip. "Pip, it's been such fun. I'm so, so glad I came! Keep in touch and I'll see you at the airport for the Forever gig. I think Flori's going to collect us in her van. Now, you'd better get those cats of yours home. I know cats are fairly nocturnal, but this is ridiculous."

Pip smiled. "Say hi to Candlemas for me."

"I surely would . . . but I didn't tell her I was coming." Star gave her a conspiratorial grin. "Bye, Sister Pip."

Pip was startled for a moment, then she realised what Star meant. They'd played aspects of the same person in *Half-Life of the Lost*. That made them sort of sisters. Maybe sisters in crime.

ABOUT THE AUTHOR

Lark Westerly loves writing series where characters weave in and out of one another's stories.

She also loves playing with ideas and notions and researching odd information.

Lark lives in the island state of Tasmania, where she walks dogs, invents recipes, and wears clothes with that lived-in look. She rarely finds a matching pair of socks.

Unlike Pippin Pearmain, Lark is not tiny, not an only child, not single and not an on-screen performer. She never learned ballet and she can't speak Cat-Morse. She doesn't even have a bucket list. Nevertheless, Pippin Pearmain and Lark Westerly are sisters under the skin.

Oh . . . you were wondering about that bucket that inspired *Performing Pippin Pearmain*? It happened like this . . .

To find out, visit https://performingpippinpearmain.weebly.com/about-the-bucket.html.